HONORS FOR APRIL HENRY

ALA Best Books for Young Adults

ALA Quick Picks for Young Adults

Barnes & Noble Top Teen Pick

Maryland Black-Eyed Susan Book Award Winner

Missouri Truman Readers Award Winner

Texas Library Association Tayshas Selection

New York Charlotte Award Winner

One Book for Nebraska Teens

Golden Sower Honor Book

Oregon Book Award

South Dakota YA Reading Program Winner

COUNT

ALL HER

BONES

COUNT

ALL HER

BONES

APRIL HENRY

Christy Ottaviano Books

Henry Holt and Company

New York

Henry Holt and Company, *Publishers since 1866*
175 Fifth Avenue, New York, New York 10010
fiercereads.com

Henry Holt® is a registered trademark of Macmillan Publishing Group, LLC.
Copyright © 2017 by April Henry

Library of Congress Cataloging-in-Publication Data is available.
ISBN 978-1-62779-591-3

Our books may be purchased in bulk for promotional, educational, or
business use. Please contact your local bookseller or the Macmillan Corporate
and Premium Sales Department at (800) 221-7945 ext. 5442 or by e-mail
at MacmillanSpecialMarkets@macmillan.com.

First edition—2017 / Design by April Ward
Printed in the United States of America

1   3   5   7   9   10   8   6   4   2

For Carlie Blazek,
who reminded me of the power
of the written word

COUNT

ALL HER

BONES

COUNT ALL OF MY BONES

A haiku by Susan Crane

Count all of my bones.
Softly lay them side by side.
Believe I mattered.

CHAPTER 1

THE TERROR, THE BRAVERY

CHEYENNE

"We only have ten days until the trial starts," Matthew Bennett said. "Do you feel ready?"

Cheyenne Wilder nodded. She heard the Multnomah County prosecutor sigh.

"When we're in court, please remember to answer out loud. All testimony is recorded."

"Okay." Cheyenne swallowed. Even though this was just practice in Mr. Bennett's office, her tongue felt too big for her mouth. What was it going to be like in the witness stand in a crowded courtroom?

She was glad he had made everyone else stay in the waiting room: Danielle; her dad, Nick; and even Jaydra, who now accompanied Cheyenne every time she left the house.

Jaydra, her bodyguard. Her keeper. Her dad said it was just until attention died down. What if someone else got it into their head to kidnap her, knowing he had already paid a million for her once?

"And keep your hands away from your mouth," Mr. Bennett said. "You need to speak clearly. The juror farthest from you should be able to hear every syllable."

Cheyenne started to nod, then caught herself. "Yes. Okay."

"And be sure not to chew gum." He hesitated. "Although, hmm, it could make you look younger. Let me think about it."

She straightened up. "Why would I want to look younger?" Because she was only five foot two, Cheyenne always sat and stood tall. She wore makeup, knowing it made her look older.

"We want the jury's sympathy." His voice firmed. "Ask your mom to pick out something that makes you look younger. Maybe something pink or with ruffles. "

Cheyenne didn't bother telling him she didn't own anything like that. Or that Danielle was her stepmom and certainly didn't pick out her clothes. She had already figured out this was a one-way conversation. Mr. Bennett wanted the jury to look at her and think she was helpless. Incapable. That she was a victim.

She hated that word.

"It's a fine line," he continued. "We want the jury to feel for you, but we also want them to trust every word you say. Initially, I'm going to take you through what happened, step by step. How you were kidnapped, how you escaped. I want them to feel the same things you did those three days. The terror of your kidnapping, the bravery of your escape."

Cheyenne hadn't felt brave, though. She shivered at the memory of running through the woods at night. Branches clawing her face. Tree roots tripping her up. Then it started to snow, adding the horrible knowledge that she must be leaving behind footprints.

"When it's the opposing counsel's turn to cross-examine you, he might ask if we've met before. It's fine to say yes. Just say I told you to tell the truth. If you tell the truth and tell it accurately, Wheeler can't cross you up. Never guess or make up an answer. If you don't know or don't remember, just say that. Answer only the exact question and then stop. For example, if I asked you how old you are, you would just say sixteen. You wouldn't tell me the time of day you were born or the name of the hospital. Don't volunteer anything."

"Okay." Cheyenne wanted to correct him, to say she would turn seventeen the day before the trial started, but Mr. Bennett didn't like interruptions. Her stomach felt queasy. What if she messed something up? What if Roy walked free? She remembered how he had howled her name as he did his best to kill her.

"That's another thing we might as well start practicing. Say 'yes, sir,' and 'no, sir,' to me and to Mr. Wheeler.

If you speak to the judge, say 'Your Honor.' And no joking around or getting agitated, even if you're feeling nervous. I'm not just talking about when you're on the stand. You need to keep it together at all times, even if you have an unexpected interaction in the hallway or outside the court-house. Your behavior could be observed and factored into the jury's decision."

Interaction in the hallway. "Are you saying I might run into Griffin?" Her stomach twisted again. She pressed her fingers to her lips.

He touched her shoulder. The surprise of it, coming out of nowhere like that, made her jerk back.

"You don't need to worry. We'll make sure he never gets anywhere near you. And you've got Ms. Hamilton to protect you, of course." He meant Jaydra.

"Have you talked to him? To Griffin?" Cheyenne managed to sound like she didn't care.

"Yes. He's in town now. We've met several times to discuss his testimony."

Her heart sped up.

"He's the one who really has to worry, not you. Wheeler's going to focus on him like a laser. He'll try to get under his skin, make him lash out. He'll argue Griffin's the one who kidnapped you. Not his father."

"But it was an accident." Cheyenne didn't know who had been more surprised when each of them figured out the other was in the car. "Griffin was just trying to steal the Escalade, not me. He saw Danielle's keys, but he didn't notice me because I was lying down in the back. And he was going to let me go. It was his father's idea to ask for the money."

Mr. Bennett made a humming noise. "We only have Griffin's word for what he would have done. James Hixon is dead, and Thomas Meadors is in a mental hospital. And even though Griffin freely admitted stealing the car, I'm sure Wheeler's going to make a big deal about his plea bargain. He'll probably claim Griffin is lying about his father's involvement in exchange for not being sent to prison as an adult." He sighed. "Wheeler's going to eat him alive on cross."

Cheyenne must have made some small sound of protest because Mr. Bennett added, "I doubt he's going to ask much of you, since the jury will see you sympathetically. The one thing he might focus on is whether you're really capable of identifying Roy as the man who told your father to pay him five million dollars or else he would send you back in pieces. He's going to say it's impossible to identify someone by only voice or scent."

"I'm blind," Cheyenne said, "not stupid. Sir."

CHAPTER 2

PLAN B

ROY

If it weren't for Cheyenne Wilder, Roy Sawyer wouldn't have been lying on the top bunk in a Multnomah County Jail cell. A cell the size of a bathroom, which he shared with a guy named Tiny. Who obviously wasn't.

Twenty-one minutes before lights-on, Roy lay curled under a blanket the color and softness of a burlap sack, trying to ignore Tiny's snores. Tap-tap-tapping on a phone. It was a smartphone that could go online, but Roy was even smarter. First was the fact he had a phone at all. He had sweet-talked it out of the new nurse, Alice, who had taken a fancy to him.

Second, Roy never actually sent any e-mail on it, even though he and his half brother shared an account. *Is everything ready?* He saved the message in the drafts folder and waited for Dwayne to read it. Once he did, Dwayne would hit the delete key.

Poof! Roy's words would be gone. Leaving no record of what had been said. What had been planned.

Then Dwayne would write his own message and save it as a draft. Which Roy would then read and delete. And so on, back and forth. A whole conversation in invisible ink.

While Roy waited for Dwayne's reply, he watched the spider on the ceiling two feet above him busily tending her web. She had set up shop a week earlier, and since then she had provided him with hours of entertainment. The spider was the first nonhuman living thing he had seen in six months.

At home, he worked outside stripping stolen cars, or in a barn with the doors standing open. Hawks wheeled overhead. At night, coyotes yipped in the woods. When Roy was arrested, it had been winter. Now everything would be in bloom, bursting with life. He was still stuck in here.

Roy checked the time. Nineteen minutes left. Just before lights-on, he would slip the phone inside a sock and tuck it in his briefs. He worked on the jail's laundry crew, so he made sure he always got the baggiest pants.

Alice had also gotten him a charger, but there were no electrical outlets inside cells. The dayroom had outlets, but it was far too open. However, the laundry room had several that could be hidden behind stacks of neatly folded uniforms.

In a few minutes, he would roll out of his bunk, pull on blue scrubs over the pink-dyed T-shirt and briefs he was already wearing. Yank on pink tube socks and stuff his feet into plastic shower shoes. The end result was that he looked more or less like everyone else. But even prison couldn't take away his tattoos. An eagle. A snake. Satan riding a Harley. Barbed wire around a heart on his biceps that also read *Janie* in flowing script. This one had caught Alice's eye. She thought it was romantic.

He even had a spider tattoo, but it was of a tarantula, not a house spider like the one above his head. His spider had delicate striped legs and a fat brown belly speckled with black.

The bunk groaned as Tiny rolled over. The jail held more than five hundred people—snoring, farting, mumbling, and bickering. For most, it was catch and release. Others, like Roy, were awaiting trial. Afterward, he would go to state prison, a place he had resolved never to go. When he got out, he would be an old man.

And what happened hadn't even been his fault. It was his boy, Griffin, who brought Cheyenne home. Roy didn't plan it. Didn't ask for it. But when the radio said this girl was the daughter of Nike's president, well, who wouldn't want a little something for her safe return? Like finding a lost cell phone and getting a reward for giving it back. He hadn't touched a hair on her head, Roy thought as he watched the spider delicately wrap up a tiny fly.

The same couldn't be said for Cheyenne. She had pressed a gun against his side and pulled the trigger. Taken out a chunk of meat just above his hip that still ached every time he lifted a load of wet uniforms. And even though she was blind, she managed to run Roy over with his own car. Now he walked with a limp.

Of course, she hadn't gotten in any trouble. No, it was Roy who was sitting here. And Griffin was walking around free. When the dummy was the one to take the girl in the first place. But he was going to get up on the stand and point his finger, run his mouth, spill his guts.

After Janie was gone, Roy had tried to raise the boy right, but obviously he'd failed. Didn't loyalty count for anything anymore? Didn't family? Dwayne wasn't even his full-blood brother, but he was willing to do whatever it took to help Roy get out of this place. Help when Roy's own son had turned against him.

Griffin. Every time Roy looked at him, he saw the boy's mother in the stubborn set of his mouth, in his dark, challenging eyes. When Griffin found out his mom was dead rather than gone, it must have turned him against Roy. And it didn't help that he had taken a fancy to Cheyenne. As if a girl like that would ever care about a guy like him.

Saw our friend in cuckoo's nest, Dwayne's last message had read. He meant TJ, who once worked for Roy. Even though he was dumber than a box of hammers, TJ had been good with tools.

TJ had been fascinated by Cheyenne. She was a little thing, even shorter than TJ. Dark curly hair, brown staring eyes. Eyes that couldn't see TJ's stupid face. Couldn't see anything.

Now TJ was in the state mental hospital, where they had filmed *One Flew Over the Cuckoo's Nest*.

The file flickered as it was replaced. When Roy opened it again, his words had been deleted and exchanged for Dwayne's. *He'll be flying free Friday. It's time for the next step bro. Ready Freddy?*

Roy took a deep breath and deleted his brother's words. His finger hesitated over the tiny keyboard. Once he pulled the trigger, there would be no going back.

It was too risky to try to escape. So he had decided to go with plan B. Make it look like the girl had run away. Without her to testify, the case would be dismissed.

But how to get to her? She had a guide dog, which Dwayne reported looked pretty tame, but still. Worse, she was accompanied by a bodyguard every time she left the house. To add insult to injury, she even had Duke in her yard, behind one of those invisible fences. Duke had once been Roy's dog.

Just like Griffin was his son. At least according to Janie. But family couldn't be a one-way street. Especially when there was a chance to kill two birds with one stone. So to speak. He began to peck out an answer.

Some choices were hard. Maybe even wrong. But they still had to be made.

Roy looked over what he had just written. After a long moment, he pressed Save.

And then he reached up with his thumb and smashed the spider against the ceiling.

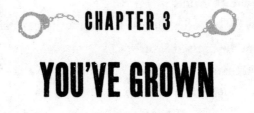

CHAPTER 3

YOU'VE GROWN

GRIFFIN

Dressed in the suit Aunt Debby had bought six months ago for his first hearing, Griffin Sawyer walked out of the bathroom at the Stay-A-While Motel.

"You've grown," Debby said. The fingers of one hand twisted through her short, dark hair. Griffin's mom, Janie, had had the same anxious habit her sister did, only her hair had been a reddish-brown waterfall to her waist.

Had he grown? He looked down. His ankles were sticking out the ends of his pants. He remembered Debby's whole family watching some awards show with pretty-boy actors on an actual red carpet. "Isn't this how guys wear suits now? Short and kind of tight?"

"Not that short and tight." She sighed. "We'll need to get you a new suit before we meet with Mr. Bennett tomorrow. We can swing by Nordstrom's Rack on the way.

Put on your regular clothes. After I take a shower, we'll go get dinner."

Great. The suit would be one more thing he would owe his aunt. After changing, he traded places with her. When the shower started, Griffin stepped outside and lit a cigarette from his hidden pack. Knowing she would probably smell it on him, but telling himself he didn't really care.

Debby hated smoking. It reminded her of his dad. Roy. She didn't get that smoking could calm you. How it gave you something to do with your hands, a place to look, an excuse to turn away every time you exhaled. How it made you feel cooler and also harder.

Cheyenne hadn't liked cigarettes either. Griffin remembered how she had yelled at him, saying he was not allowed to smoke in her stepmom's car. His lips quirked at the memory. As if it didn't matter she was tied up with her own shoelaces in the back of the car.

She was more free tied up than Griffin had ever been just walking around.

But somehow, being around her had made him more free. With Cheyenne, he became a different person. Smarter. Braver. Brave enough to risk helping her escape.

He kicked an empty McDonald's cup and sent it rolling across the parking lot. His life was so much better now. Wasn't it? That's what everyone kept telling him. He lived with Aunt Debby and Uncle Jeff in Chicago, not with a dad who ran an illegal chop shop and who'd hit you as soon as look at you. And Debby loved him. At least she said she did. Maybe it had been easier to love Griffin when he was eight, which was the last time they had seen each other until six months ago.

So why was he still screwing up? In a few weeks, unless he managed to snag the mail first, Debby would get his report card and realize he'd flunked all his classes, mostly because he had just stopped going.

At his new school, he'd gotten lost in the shuffle. Everyone there had problems. Pregnant girls and drug addicts and kids who were both. Griffin wasn't the only one who struggled with reading, or was more than a year behind in school, or caught up in the justice system. Even the teachers were screwups. They left only a couple of messages about his absences, which he erased before Debby heard them.

Every day it took more and more effort to go, until finally he just stopped walking in the front doors and started walking around the city instead, his little sketch-book in his back pocket. He sketched people he saw—a young mom holding a sleeping baby, an old drunk stretched out on a park bench, a guy walking five tiny dogs.

And even though Griffin told himself to stop, that it was pointless to keep torturing himself, his most frequent subject was Cheyenne. Her heart-shaped face. Her dark eyes. Her smile and how it turned up higher at one corner.

When he was with her, it seemed like he could be a better person. Someone who wasn't just a thief. Someone who knew more than how to break into cars, how to steal them, how to part them out. Someone better than his dad.

But that feeling had ended six months ago, when he risked calling Cheyenne from Chicago. When he asked if they could keep in touch.

In the woods, he had been willing to die for her. But when he called, her answer had been no.

No.

That "no" still played in an endless loop in his head. Had her voice hitched a little? Were her parents watching? Had they made her say that?

Now they were only a few miles apart. Griffin threw down his cigarette and crushed it under his heel. His chest hurt like something was stuck inside, taking up the space his lungs needed. As soon as the trial ended, he would be back in Chicago, thousands of miles away. He'd probably never see her again.

Not that he would see her here. The prosecutor, Bennett, had made that clear, his blue eyes boring into him. As if he could see Griffin thinking that Cheyenne must have been there before him, breathing the same air. As if he could tell how much Griffin longed to see her, even once.

Bennett had made him a deal. Tell the truth about what his dad had done, about what all of them had done, and his dad would go to prison while Griffin would be free.

But free to do what?

CHAPTER 4

SUPPOSED TO BE THE VICTIM

CHEYENNE

Cheyenne was brushing her teeth when she heard movement behind her. Maybe it wasn't even a sound that alerted her but the air shifting. A second later, an arm slid across her throat.

She dropped her toothbrush and tried to spin away. Too late. The arm yanked her back in. A grunt in her ear. The heat of her attacker's body against her back as the arm began to tighten.

Cheyenne knew how it would go down. Once pressure was applied to the carotid arteries, she'd be unconscious within ten seconds. And it wouldn't take much longer to kill her.

She could try to claw the eyes, but her attacker's cheek was pressed tight against her shoulder blades. Try to shift her hips and go for the groin, hoping to at least loosen the grip. But if that didn't work, there wouldn't be time to try something else.

Her attacker probably hoped she would go down without much of a fight.

Oh, hell to the no. Cheyenne curled her fingers over the arm and yanked, letting her legs go boneless. As she dropped, she twisted, rolling her attacker over her hip. No sounds except for their ragged breathing. But that was enough for Phantom to know something was wrong. Out in the hall, he scratched at the bedroom door her attacker had closed and then began to bark in sharp, staccato bursts. The chances anyone would hear him were small. Mary, their cook and housekeeper, had already gone home. Her dad was in Japan. And Danielle was volunteering at an evening clinic.

Cheyenne managed to stay on her feet, still holding the arm she had grabbed straight up. As her attacker fell, it twisted nearly to the breaking point. She turned her head, and there it was, a pale, blurry line in the tiny slice of vision she had left. She dropped her knees, one on her attacker's head, the other on the ribs, and began to inch the arm back, back, back. Finding the point where it would snap.

"Tap!" Jaydra grunted.

Cheyenne let go and straightened up.

"You were smiling," Jaydra said as she got to her feet.

"Sorry." Feeling her face warm, Cheyenne went to the door and let Phantom in.

"No, the smile was a nice touch," Jaydra said. "A bad guy is going to think twice or even three times if he sees the person who's supposed to be the victim smiling."

Phantom let out one last woof as Cheyenne rubbed the fur behind his ears. She wondered what he thought of Jaydra. Around other people, he would curl up and nap if he wasn't needed. But with Jaydra, he was always alert.

"That was very good," Jaydra continued. "You never stopped moving. And you didn't end up on the bottom. I only weigh one-forty. If some guy weighs two-forty, it won't matter how many locks and chokes you know. You let him get his weight on you and he won't even have to know jujitsu."

"I don't know why I have to worry about this." Cheyenne shook her head. "Phantom will protect me." Hearing his name, he pressed against her thigh. Part of her was braced for Jaydra to come back at her. She liked to spring things on you when you least expected it. Just like she had three minutes ago, when she had come over from the guesthouse and slipped into Cheyenne's room.

"He's a guide dog. Not a guard dog. He's not bred for it, and he's not trained for it. He's not like Duke." Duke had once been Roy's dog, and as a result, he had some issues. Still, he had helped Cheyenne escape, and she had returned the favor by taking him in.

"But Phantom is smart. Like, if I tell him to cross the street and can't hear that an electric car is coming, he won't move, even though he's supposed to obey me." It was called intelligent disobedience. "So why couldn't he learn to be a guard dog?"

"Not crossing when an electric car is coming is a lot different from deciding whom you're going to bite and whom you're going to ignore. And he can't both guide you and guard you. Even if he tried, that harness is going to get in his way. And what if they lock him in a car? Or hurt him? Even kill him? You can't rely on anyone but yourself to get you out of trouble."

For the past six months, Jaydra had been not just Cheyenne's bodyguard but her trainer. After Nick had hired her to watch over Cheyenne, Jaydra had sold him on also teaching Cheyenne how to protect herself. It was like the orientation and mobility training she had right after the accident, except this focused solely on dealing with bad guys. How to keep safe at the ATM, on public transportation, walking in an iffy neighborhood. What to do if someone grabbed your wrist, your neck, around your waist.

And how to fight back. A sighted person could run away, but a blind person needed to disable their attacker. As long as Cheyenne had contact with her partner, she didn't need to see to use jujitsu. Could be, according to Jaydra, as good as a sighted person. Since she couldn't watch Jaydra's moves, Cheyenne had learned how to kick, punch, and flip people by feeling the position of Jaydra's body and then copying it herself. They practiced in the home gym, which had been reconfigured with mats covering the hardwood floors and even two of the walls. Sometimes Jaydra attacked her with a plastic training gun or a training knife that lacked an edge on the blade.

Cheyenne had never seen anything but a blurry sideways slice of Jaydra. Three years ago, two cars had been racing down a country road, the same road she and her mom were walking on. Then an oncoming car made the driver in the wrong lane swerve onto the shoulder—and right into them. Her mom had been killed, and Cheyenne had been thrown into a sign. The impact bounced her brain off the back of her skull. While her eyes still worked, the part of her brain that took in the message had been destroyed. The car accident had spared only the far-left edge of her old field of vision, and even that was fuzzy and unfocused. From that, she knew Jaydra had pale skin and long, dark hair. In her imagination, the other woman's eyes were blue. That part she would never know, unless she asked. Her slice of sight wasn't even enough to tell her that Jaydra wore her hair pulled back into a tight braid. Her fingers knew, though. It was useful for yanking when Cheyenne could get past her own reluctance to fight dirty.

Jaydra was all about fighting dirty, if it let you live. All about improvising with what you had on hand. Anything and everything could be a weapon. A phone could be smashed across the bridge of a nose. A pen could stab an eye or the throat. A bag of groceries could be shoved into someone's arms—and then Cheyenne could attack while they fumbled. Even an empty hand could be slapped across the ear, damaging the ear drum.

That thought made Cheyenne shiver. To be blind and deaf? She had met a few people like that, and while they seemed to have adjusted, to her it would be like being locked in a box forever.

"At the end, you twisted your head," Jaydra said. "You need to forget about that little bit you can see. It won't help, and it puts you in a bad position versus your attacker."

"Okay." Cheyenne repressed a sigh. Nothing she did was ever good enough. She could probably kill Jaydra, and the other woman would manage to come back from the dead to critique her technique.

Still, Cheyenne liked grappling. It made her feel bad-ass. Like a ninja warrior.

At the same time, it was overkill. Her dad and step-mom had turned paranoid and protective. Cheyenne had lost count of the times Danielle had apologized for leaving Cheyenne alone in the Escalade.

But she hadn't been the target. The car had. It was just a fluke Griffin hadn't noticed her until it was too late. A once-in-a-lifetime thing.

Cheyenne couldn't wait for the trial to end. Until then, she joked to her friend Kenzie, she was just lucky Jaydra was staying in the guesthouse instead of in a bunk bed in Cheyenne's room.

Every weekday, Jaydra took Cheyenne to her private school and then picked her up to take her straight home again. Her dad would no longer let Cheyenne go out to movies or concerts or even to friends' houses. If she wanted to hang out with someone, he said she should just ask them over. If she wanted to go shopping, he said she could have things shipped to her and return those she didn't want.

She felt like she was slowly suffocating. At home it was so quiet. Danielle had her volunteer work, and her dad was always traveling. Some weeks Cheyenne talked to Mary or the gardener, Octavio, more than she talked to her parents. Of course there was Jaydra, but conversations with her tended to be more like lectures. While she could text or call her friends, that wasn't the same as being with them. And even though Kenzie and Sadie would come over if she asked, it didn't change the fact that she was still stuck at home.

"It won't be long until the trial starts," Cheyenne said now. "Once Roy is sentenced, my parents won't have to worry anymore."

Jaydra made a noncommittal grunt.

Cheyenne tensed. "What?"

"It's not only Roy that Nick's worried about. It's anyone with a cell phone. Anyone who looks at you and sees dollar signs. You're not exactly incognito. You're pretty and petite, so I'm sure guys were already noticing you. Now everyone recognizes you, especially given you always have a cane or a dog. Do you know how many stories have been written about you? I don't mean just *People* magazine. I'm talking tabloids, blog posts, Twitter, Tumblr. Your family has been wanting to shield you from it, but there are a lot of crazies out there. Hiding behind made-up names, anonymous IP addresses. And some of them want to do more than just take your picture."

After Jaydra left, Cheyenne searched for her own name on Twitter. And was immediately sorry after her computer read her the first leering remark.

"I'd like to tie her up and hold her for ransom."

And that was mild compared to the rest. Her stomach crammed into the back of her throat as she slammed her laptop closed.

Would she ever get her life back?

CHAPTER 5

BUILDING THE GIRL PIECE BY PIECE

TJ

TJ Meadors lay in his narrow bed in the room he shared with five other men at the Oregon State Hospital and thought about Cheyenne Wilder.

His lips moved as he softly said her name. Even saying it out loud, it still sounded like a whisper. He imagined tucking her long, dark hair behind her ear. Breathing "Cheyenne" into that white shell.

Only this time she wouldn't flinch.

TJ spent as much time with Cheyenne as he could, even if it was only in his head. It helped him block out reality, like the snoring and mumbling around him. And later, when lights suddenly ripped open the night just so a staff member could untangle a headphone cord from around one of TJ's stupid roommates' heads, he pulled the blanket over his face and remembered.

Thoughts of Cheyenne helped him ignore how the

blanket smelled like disinfectant and the pillow was as hard as a board. He just kept his eyes closed tight and filled his senses with memories of her, building the girl piece by piece. Her soft, pale skin. Her sweet smell, like something precious and expensive. Her dark sightless eyes that had looked right at him but never seen him.

Two weeks ago, Dwayne, Roy's half brother, had visited, promising that TJ could see Cheyenne again. Do more than see her, if he wanted.

On the grounds, they sat in white plastic lawn chairs, away from the others. TJ ate chip after chip from the two bags of Ruffles Cheddar & Sour Cream Dwayne bought from the vending machine.

"Easy there, eager beaver," Dwayne said. Roy was thin as a snake, but Dwayne was bulked up, with tattoos crawling up his thick arms. "You might want to think about chewing."

"It just tastes so good. The chow here sucks." Somehow the food service department was able to mess up anything, even spaghetti, but you still had to eat it.

"You always wear a jacket like that?" Dwayne eyed TJ's brown puffer coat, one of the few things he really owned. Underneath he wore "state clothes," which were the cheapest sweatpants, T-shirt, underwear, and socks available.

TJ hunched his shoulders despite the sunshine. "I get cold." He was always cold now. Jimbo was the one who used to complain about how he was freezing, who dressed in layers until he looked like the Michelin Man. Had some part of Jimbo slipped into TJ after he squeezed the trigger?

"My brother said you liked Cheyenne."

TJ smiled. "She's pretty." He used to have a picture of her, torn from *People* magazine (headline: KIDNAPPED BLIND TEEN ESCAPES ABDUCTORS!). He had kept it under his T-shirt, close to his heart, until a nurse found it and took it away.

"I know what you're thinkin', Abe Lincoln. The trial's gonna be happening soon. She's testifying against Roy."

TJ shrugged. Nobody was calling him to testify. Not from this place.

"How'd you like to be with her again? Be all lovey-dovey?"

Even though he wanted it to be true, TJ knew enough to be wary. People didn't offer you good stuff for free. "How could that even happen?" He reached up to stroke his rat tail, until he remembered how they had cut it off that first day and then buzzed his head in a room that smelled eye-wateringly of bleach.

Dwayne looked around the yard, which was filled with a half dozen guards and more than a hundred patients. Only they weren't patients. They were prisoners, just like TJ. "Say you could get out of here and go to her. Would you?"

"Yeah, but that's never gonna happen." The hope that fluttered in his chest stilled. There were no bars on the windows here, but there might as well be. Every unit had a locked door. Even if you got through that, the stairs and elevators couldn't be entered without a security badge. And the only exit required passing through not one but two locked gates.

"Never say never. In a couple days, you might get a little present."

TJ still wasn't following. "Are you going to bring Cheyenne here?"

A look of impatience crossed Dwayne's face, so for a moment he looked more like Roy. "No. But I can help you go to her. Every time they let you out into the yard, start pulling a chair right up to the fence."

"And do what?"

"Just link your fingers in the chain links and stare out. And that's all you do. Every day. Pretty soon they won't care, because they'll figure they don't need to. They won't even really see you. The way a place like this works is that they focus on people who're trouble. They're not gonna care about you sitting here doing nothing." Dwayne smiled. One of his eyeteeth was gray. "And then one day soon, you'll just go—poof!"

CHAPTER 6

FLY UNDER THE RADAR

GRIFFIN

The only good thing about a dress shirt, Griffin thought as he fumbled with the buttons in the changing room, was it mostly covered up the scar wrapped around his throat. He hated summers because the scar was so much harder to hide. Cheyenne knew about his scar, but she was the only person he had met who wouldn't flinch if he took off his shirt.

Since you couldn't outgrow a tie, Griffin had brought the one he'd worn to the original hearing into the dressing room, along with the new suit and shirt. He didn't know how to tie it, so he carefully slipped it over his head before tightening the existing knot Uncle Jeff had made six months ago.

Next, he shrugged on the suit jacket. In his reflection, Griffin saw both his dad and his mom. His dad in his narrow lips, his mom in his sad, dark brown eyes. So which one did he take after? The criminal or the victim?

He walked out of the changing area and took a deep breath.

"Do you like that one? It looks good on you." Debby nodded, agreeing with herself. The suit was a blue so dark it was almost black. She adjusted a seam on his shoulder, smoothed down his lapels. "And you can wear it to your mom's service as well as to court. Oh, Griffin, I wish Janie could see you all grown up." She slipped her arms around him.

He let her hug him, trying not to stiffen. It was his fault his mom was dead.

When he was ten, Griffin had startled his dad when he was cooking out in the barn. Not food, but meth. When it flared up, it caught Griffin's shirt on fire. A month in the burn unit followed. In his nightmares, the nurses in their blue plastic gowns and rubber gloves were wheeling him to the debridement room to scrub off his dead flesh with wire-bristled brushes.

While he was in the hospital, his parents fought over what had happened. Roy shoved his mom, and Janie fell and didn't get up. He claimed to have thought she was dead drunk, at least until the next morning. By that point she was simply dead. He had buried her out back.

After the truth came out six months ago, the authorities had dug his mom up and then conducted an autopsy on what was left of her remains. None of her bones, including her skull, were broken. Without a clear cause of death, they decided it was too hard to prosecute Roy, even as they went after him for Cheyenne's kidnapping.

Debby had arranged for a small memorial service Saturday, the day after tomorrow. It had made sense to wait until both of them would be back in town for the trial. His mom had already been dead for nearly eight years, so Debby said a few more months wouldn't matter. Griffin wondered if there was anyone left in Portland who remembered her.

Debby interrupted his thoughts. "Why don't you wear the suit out of the store. It makes you look so grown-up."

He did as she suggested, carrying himself a little taller. When they walked into the prosecutor's office, Bennett cocked his head.

"New suit?"

"He outgrew the old one," she explained.

One side of his mouth went up in what might have been a smile. "You should probably take off that tag before going to court."

Following the prosecutor's pointing finger, Griffin twisted his left wrist. A square white tag was stapled at the back. No wonder people had looked at him as they walked back to the car. Not with admiration, but because he looked like an idiot. His neck went hot as he tried to get it off, but he didn't have any fingernails left. Aunt

Debby grabbed his wrist and started picking at it while the flush climbed up his face.

Opening a drawer, Bennett handed Griffin a pen and a yellow legal pad.

"What are these for?"

"So you can take notes. I need to prepare you for what we are likely to face next week. No matter what the crime is, there are really only two defenses." He held up one finger. "I didn't do it, or"—he added a second finger—"I did it, but it was for a reason. It would be difficult for your father to say he didn't do it, as he was arrested at the scene, although I guess Wheeler could try to claim he was there for some benign purpose. But it's much more likely your father will say that not only did you take Cheyenne, but it was your idea to hold her for ransom."

Griffin let out a startled laugh. "What, like I was the boss of my dad?" He could just imagine how Roy would have reacted to that idea. Not with words but with his fists.

"Your father's going to claim you're the real mastermind."

Feeling Bennett's eyes on him, Griffin wrote down *master mind*. At least it was easy to spell. He had a million tricks to make it look like he knew what he was doing. And his memory was good. It helped fill in the gaps, hide how hard it was for him to read.

Every time Bennett said "father," Griffin had to think

who he meant. *Father* was a word from a different world, a world where the dad put on a suit and tie like the ones Griffin was now wearing, went to work, and then came home and helped his children with homework.

Griffin stated the obvious. "My dad would never let anyone tell him what to do."

"You've got a few inches on him now, so the jury might not see that." Last winter, Griffin and Roy had been eye to eye. The idea of being bigger than his dad gave Griffin a secret thrill. "And you have a history of violence."

"History of violence?" Bennett must be talking about his dad.

"You've been in at least two altercations at school since you moved to Chicago."

Griffin groaned. "I didn't *fight*. I fought back." He had tried to explain the difference to Debby and Jeff, and he thought she, at least, believed him. Still, the last one had gotten him a three-day suspension.

"Be that as it may, the defense will bring it up, as well as anything else Wheeler can throw at you. He'll try to get under your skin. Don't get angry. Don't make a bad impression."

"Okay." Griffin's shoulders hunched. If Bennett knew about the fights at school, did he also know Griffin had stopped going altogether?

The prosecutor was still looking at him expectantly,

so he put pen to paper again. But he angled it so no one could see what he was doing. In a few lines, he began to capture Cheyenne's face.

"It's going to be very uncomfortable on that stand. Your dad is going to be staring at you from the defense table. You'll find it easier if you don't make eye contact."

Griffin nodded. He would much rather be with Cheyenne than in this room with a man naming all his problems and faults. He sketched in her eyes that tipped up just a little at the corners.

"But what about how Roy gave Griffin third-degree burns?" Aunt Debby demanded. "What about how he killed my sister?"

"Wheeler could spin those burns as a reason for Griffin framing his father. And Mr. Sawyer's only on trial for what he did to Cheyenne Wilder, not what he did to Griffin or his mother." Bennett turned to Griffin. "If you stick to the facts and don't let your emotions get the better of you, your dad will be put away for years. You'll never have to worry about him again."

Last month, Uncle D. had called Griffin. Begged him not to say anything. Ordered him not to. "Look, this is your dad we're talking about." His uncle's voice was tight. "If it weren't for him, you wouldn't even exist. You owe him that much."

Griffin tried to make his voice firm. "I'm not going to lie."

Uncle D. had sighed in exasperation. "And I'm not asking you to lie. I'm asking you to not remember. Nobody likes a snitch."

Now Griffin felt like he was being picked at from all sides. Get justice for Cheyenne. Get revenge for his mom and for himself. Remember that his dad was still his dad. Tell the truth. Forget the truth.

Even without his testimony, wouldn't the government have more than enough evidence to convict his dad?

He tried to imagine what would happen after the trial was over. Going back to a city where he knew no one and had no friends. Where Uncle Jeff always seemed to look at him with narrowed eyes. Where there was no chance of ever seeing Cheyenne again. He added the sharp angle of her jaw to his sketch, and a few squiggles to suggest her curly hair. Even looking at the paper version of her made his heart fill with longing.

When he turned eighteen, would Aunt Debby cut him loose?

What if he just took off before the trial? Let fate decide what happened to Roy? There were lots of jobs where they paid in cash and didn't ask for any ID. He was pretty sure he looked older than he was, or at least he would when his hair grew out a little bit from the military-style cut Uncle Jeff had insisted on.

But Griffin's own plea bargain wouldn't stand if he didn't testify. Then the government could charge him—would charge him, according to Bennett—as an adult.

But that was if they caught him. And if Roy had taught Griffin anything, it was how to fly under the radar.

CHAPTER 7

SUCH A FINAL WORD

CHEYENNE

"One message in Other folder," Cheyenne's computer said in its speeded-up voice. It was the end of the day, and she was stretched out on her bed, using her laptop keyboard to move around Facebook. The house was quiet. Phantom lay dozing at her feet. Guide dogs were trained to stay off furniture, but Cheyenne had long ago made an exception for her bed.

The Other folder? There was never anything in that folder. She was pretty sure it was for messages that didn't come from friends. Because she didn't want her dad and Danielle to find out about the account, her user name was Phantom Smith and she kept her friends list small.

Maybe it was a birthday message from someone at school. Some birthday this would be. Her dad and Danielle didn't even want to go out to dinner. They said she could have friends over for a party after the trial was over.

Before clicking on the message, she checked out who it was from. A guy, but no one she knew. He lived in Los Angeles. Seventeen, named Hunter Forest. They had one friend in common—Kenzie, who had been friends with Cheyenne forever. But Kenzie had never mentioned anyone named Hunter Forest. Then again, Kenzie had over six hundred Facebook friends.

Cheyenne clicked.

"Just like Phantom isn't you, Hunter isn't me. I'm in town from Chicago and then I'll never come back to Portland. But I keep thinking that we're not very far apart."

Cheyenne's breath caught. Even though her computer's current voice was female, even though the message came from someone calling himself Hunter Forest, she knew who had written those words. Griffin Sawyer. The last time they had been together, they were on the run in the woods. Or hunted in the forest.

Six months ago, Griffin had called and asked if they could keep in touch. Taking a deep breath, Cheyenne thought about what her dad and Danielle had said. Just because Griffin helped her get away, that really didn't change who he was. What he was. A dropout. A thief. A smoker. (For Danielle, a nurse, smoking was on par with the worst of sins.) Griffin, they said, was the son of a criminal, brought up to follow in his footsteps. They made it clear that Cheyenne and Griffin could never be friends.

So Cheyenne said no.

But that hadn't stopped her from thinking about him ever since.

Cheyenne still saw things with her mind's eye, even things she had never seen before the accident. So she had taken the bits of Griffin she had collected in the nearly three days they were together and fashioned them into a whole three-dimensional person. When he first stole Danielle's Escalade, they struggled. From that she knew he was strong, corded with muscle. And that he was taller than her—although pretty much everyone was. Later, when they were just beginning to form an uneasy alliance, they took turns describing each other. She had guessed he had dark hair, and the way he had sucked in his breath said she was right. She imagined him with dark eyes as well. Some of the pieces were less tangible, like the slightly spicy way Griffin smelled, a mix of tobacco and something sharper. Or how he caught his breath that one time she turned and they were only inches apart.

She imagined him now, lifting one dark eyebrow, waiting for her answer, his head cocked, his eyes both wary and hopeful.

She should just delete the message. Maybe her whole Facebook page. Her fingers trembled faintly against the keys.

Instead Cheyenne clicked to replay it.

". . . *never come back to Portland.*" Never was such a final word. She remembered what it was like to realize she would never see her mom again. Never talk to her. Never hug her. Even now the grief could still catch her like a kick to the gut.

Not giving herself time to think about whether it was a good idea, Cheyenne typed in her answer.

"I don't think we're supposed to be talking to each other. Because of the trial."

After she hit Send, she checked her Braille watch. Griffin had written the note more than an hour ago. How long would it take him to reply? She jumped when Phantom snorted in his sleep. In case Danielle decided to stop by to say good night, Cheyenne put in her headphones. She didn't want to answer any questions about whose message she was listening to.

Even though it seemed like forever, Griffin answered within a few minutes. "If no one knows about it, how can it hurt anything? Besides, I don't want to talk about the trial. I just want to talk to you."

Cheyenne would rather talk to someone on the computer or phone, because then they both had exactly the same amount of information. Face-to-face, a sighted person could look at her expression, her body language, even how she dressed, and already know far more about her than she did about them, with only her ears to rely on. But a message or a phone call made them equals.

"I guess that's okay. How did you find me?" Waiting for his reply, she wiped her damp hands on the quilt covering the bed. It was called a crazy quilt because it was made of scraps. Her mom's grandmother had made it in the 1930s. In her memory, Cheyenne could still see its blues, greens, and purples, and how all the different colors and patterns somehow came together to make a beautiful whole.

"I couldn't find you at first. Then I remembered you talking about Kenzie. When I saw Phantom Smith on her list of friends, I knew," Griffin wrote. "I've been thinking a lot. About what happened. And about you. Those 3 days were so intense. When I was with you, I felt alive."

Her heart sped up. She remembered talking with him about things she never told anyone. Remembered the sound of his laugh, the press of his fingers when he led her from place to place. Cheyenne had found a new self with Griffin, too. One who wasn't so afraid. Wasn't so angry at how everything had changed. One who finally said goodbye to the past and started walking toward her future. Even if it was a future she would never see with her own eyes.

"I've been thinking a lot about you, too," she admitted. Feeling unsure of what to type next, she switched to a safer topic. "How are things in Chicago?"

"Muggy. I miss Oregon."

Griffin had been taken in by his mom's sister. "And your family?"

"I haven't talked to my dad since he was arrested."

The mention of Roy reminded Cheyenne that Griffin would always be his father's son. "I meant your aunt and uncle."

"Ok. Don't think they trust me, though. I get lonely." He added, "That's why I really want to see you. I liked who I was with you."

Six months ago, Cheyenne had managed to make it out of the woods with nothing but first Duke and then a broken branch and the light of the rising sun to guide her. Griffin had tracked her down, not to kill her, as she first thought, but to help her.

Still, that was then. This was now. Even though she had spent the last six months replaying every interaction between them. Even though she kept wishing she had said yes to him when he called.

"I wish I could, but it's just not possible." Her keystrokes came slower and slower. "I probably shouldn't even be talking to you."

Now her dad and Danielle acted like she was a doll too precious to be played with. A doll that sat in a display case.

"All I'm asking is one time. Just one."

She swallowed, her mouth suddenly dry. "I really want to, but there's no way I can. My dad and Danielle are paranoid. They don't let me go anywhere but school.

I even have a bodyguard!" Just typing the word *bodyguard* made her feel ridiculous.

Everyone had made a million rules for her.

Maybe it was time to intelligently disobey them.

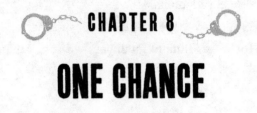

CHAPTER 8

ONE CHANCE

CHEYENNE

"Let's go out to lunch," Cheyenne said to Kenzie as they walked out of language arts. She was still buzzing from messaging back and forth with Griffin the night before.

Kenzie had a car, and before Jaydra had started taking Cheyenne to and from school, Kenzie had often driven her.

"I thought you weren't allowed to leave campus anymore." Catlin Gabel, a small private school, was a tucked-away oasis that looked like a college campus.

Cheyenne gritted her teeth. "I'm tired of only doing the things I'm allowed to."

Kenzie, who had always been more of a free spirit, clapped her hands. "Yes! I've been waiting for you to say that. So are we going to badge out?"

"Hell, no."

Juniors and seniors were allowed to go off campus for lunch, but they were supposed to run their ID badge past a card reader on their way in and out. Like most systems, however, it relied on people actually using it.

Kenzie opened the back door of her car for Phantom. "Where do you want to go?"

"I don't care. A drive-through." Just in case a teacher or administrator happened by, Cheyenne folded forward on the seat, waiting to sit up until she was sure the car was off campus. "Griffin sent me a message on Facebook," she said as she straightened up.

Kenzie snapped off the music. "Are you serious?"

"It's all thanks to you. The two of you have been Facebook friends since last week."

"I don't think so." The tick of the turn signal filled the car. "I would for sure notice that name."

"He's using the name Hunter Forest. But it's definitely Griffin."

"You mean that cute guy on the surfboard?" Kenzie sounded disappointed. "I guess I should have known he was too good to be true."

"I can't see photos, remember?" These days, Cheyenne had only her memories to guide her as to which actors, singers, or guys at school were cute. Since she had lost her sight, more and more people were attractive because of the way they acted, not the way they looked. "But yeah, I'll bet that was just a photo off the Internet. If you didn't recognize him, why did you accept his friend request?"

"He didn't live here, so I figured I didn't have to worry about what he was like in real life. It's fun to have friends in other states. I usually say yes unless they look like a creeper. And of course if anyone ever got weird, I would block them."

"Well, after you said yes to him, he was able to send me a message because we had you in common."

"But you're not even you on Facebook."

"Using Phantom's name and photo is not much of a disguise," Cheyenne pointed out. Kenzie had helped her set up the account, even taken Phantom's picture. The only time Cheyenne took pictures now was when she was using an app for the blind that could tell her the color of a sweater or what was inside a can in the cupboard. "Anyway, Griffin's in town for the trial. And he wants to see me." Just saying the words out loud made a thrill race through her.

With a squeal, Kenzie clutched Cheyenne's arm. "That's so romantic!"

"Part of me agrees with you," Cheyenne said. "But part of me thinks it's crazy to even think about it." Her head and heart were warring with each other. Her dad had always trusted her. But what if this was her last chance to see Griffin?

"Look at everything he did for you, though. He helped

you run away from his dad and those two crazy guys. Even after you tried to kill him!" Kenzie's voice rose and fell with passion. "And then when he broke his ankle, he told you to go on without him."

And all Griffin was asking in return was for one meeting, Cheyenne thought as the car slowed and then went over a speed bump. She and Griffin had seen the best and worst of each other. They had experienced more in three days than most couples would in a lifetime. For the past six months, she had bottled up her feelings, but now that they were unstoppered, the idea of never seeing him again was devastating.

Kenzie's window hummed down. Outside the car, a voice crackled. "May I take your order?"

"Yeah," Kenzie said. "Two chocolate peanut butter shakes, two large orders of fries, and a Tillamook Cheeseburger with bacon." It was their standard order at Burgerville. The cheeseburger was half for Cheyenne and half for Phantom. Kenzie had been a vegetarian since third grade. She paid and pulled forward to wait for their food.

"The problem is, I don't see how it's possible. I'm never alone. If I absolutely have to go someplace, it's with my dad or Danielle or Jaydra—or all three."

Kenzie poked her side. "Said the girl who's sitting in a Burgerville drive-through with no adults in sight. I could be your getaway driver. I could take you from school to wherever he is."

The cashier handed over their order, and the car filled with the intoxicating scent of French fries, bacon, and freshly cooked meat. Kenzie pulled into a shaded corner of the lot, rolled down the windows, and turned off the engine.

As she took a bite of her burger, Cheyenne mulled the idea.

"You'd have a three-hour window between lunch and last period. Or"—Kenzie drew out the word as she thought—"Jaydra drops you off, you meet me in the student parking lot, and we leave. That would give you the whole day."

"Either way, school would call home when we didn't show up in class." Cheyenne ripped off a chunk of burger and passed it back to Phantom. "And then we'd be screwed."

"You know I can speak adult. I'll call in for both of us." Kenzie lowered her voice and spoke quickly, sounding like a harried businesswoman. " 'I'm afraid Cheyenne won't be in today. She's come down with a touch of food poisoning.' And then I'll call back again for me, but with a different excuse. I'll drop you off at school right before it ends, and you can meet Jaydra at the pickup area like you just got out of class."

"It could work. Or it could totally fall apart. And then I'll be grounded forever."

"Face it. You already *are* grounded." Kenzie noisily

sucked up the last of her shake. "How much more could they take away from you?"

"Right now, at least nobody's following me around at school. If they find out, I'm going to get in so much trouble. Jaydra would probably never let me out of her sight again."

"The guys would love it if she came to school," Kenzie said. "She's like an assassin. They'll all be busy guessing where she hides her gun or asking her to cuff them."

When her dad had said he was hiring a bodyguard for her, Cheyenne had imagined some beefy, burly guy with a shaved head. Some no-nonsense ex-military dude who could barely fit his shoulders into a jacket. What she got was Jaydra. Her dad said he wanted someone who could follow her into the ladies' room without raising eyebrows.

"She's basically like a babysitter."

"A tattooed babysitter who knows jujitsu and who gives you pointers about how to get out of handcuffs," Kenzie said. "Besides, even if they catch us, we could always make up some lie about why we left. We could say we wanted to go shopping or something. We won't tell them you saw Griffin, and we'll make sure he doesn't tell anyone. And once the trial is over, your parents will relax."

Cheyenne took a deep breath. "I'm going to tell him yes."

Kenzie squealed and squeezed her hand with greasy fingers.

Cheyenne hadn't really been paying attention to the sounds outside their windows, but now she heard a woman say, "Look at that dog! It is her, like I told you. Hey, Cheyenne, look over here! Cheyenne!"

A second voice, a man's. "Are you ready for the trial, Cheyenne?" He sounded closer than the woman.

Cheyenne shrank back. "Are they reporters?" If they were, she would never be alone again.

Kenzie swore. Like Cheyenne, she no longer trusted reporters. "I think they're just people. Nosy people." The car started up and jerked into reverse. "They're standing right behind the car." The pitch of her voice changed as she leaned out the window to yell, "Move your butts before I run you over!"

Cheyenne ducked her head and put her hand over her face as Kenzie squealed out of the lot. Had she just blown her one chance to see Griffin?

CHAPTER 9

PHYSICAL PROBLEMS WITH PHYSICAL SOLUTIONS

CHEYENNE

Cheyenne's outing to Burgerville had not leaked into the wider world. At least not yet. She had set up a Google Alert to see if anyone posted photos of her out and about when she was supposed to be in lockdown at school. So far, nothing new had shown up.

Now she sat in the passenger seat of the Escalade, lost in thought as Jaydra drove home from school. In just three days, she could be seeing Griffin. Where would they meet? What would they do? They would have at least seven hours together.

"You sound happy," Jaydra said. It seemed as much a question as an observation.

Cheyenne froze. She had been running her index finger over her lower lip, wondering what it might be like to kiss Griffin. "What?"

"You were humming."

"Oh, um, Kenzie had me listen to this new band she likes." To forestall any questions about the imaginary band, she changed the subject. "It must be getting kind of boring, just driving me back and forth to school."

"You can't let yourself think like that. That's when you start making mistakes. I don't know if you've noticed, but I try to pick a different route each time. It keeps me from getting bored, and it keeps us from being predictable. Predictability is what gets people killed."

"What do you mean?" Cheyenne asked, mostly to keep her talking. It wasn't hard. Jaydra liked to lecture. How adrenaline affected your body. How when seconds counted, the police were minutes away. How movement was life, because movement indicated initiative. And whoever had the initiative won the battle. Meanwhile, Cheyenne could continue to internally debate whether she should wear perfume Monday.

"There was a high-level executive in New York who always used to go to the same diner for breakfast. He was kidnapped walking back to his car. Another guy used to stop every morning at the end of his gated driveway to get the paper. The neighbors found his car still running—with the driver's door open. Only he was gone."

A shiver crept across Cheyenne's skin. What good was life if you had to worry every time you left your house? "So if you were the bodyguard for one of those guys—

what? You wouldn't let them eat at their favorite restaurant? You wouldn't let them get the paper?"

"Maybe I'd be the one to get the paper. And if my client really, really wanted to eat at that restaurant, I'd insist on accompanying him. And see if I could secure a parking spot for us right outside the door. Entrance and egress—leaving—are the most dangerous points of any travel plan. That's why I don't let you get out of the car until we're right in front of the school."

Cheyenne most definitely did not want Jaydra thinking about her safety at school. What if she took it into her head to begin following Cheyenne from class to class? "You seem like you know a lot, so how come you're not guarding an ambassador or a movie star or something? Instead of just me?"

"When it comes to personal protection, it's still a man's world." Jaydra let out a huff. "Most people won't hire a woman for a high-profile job. Everyone's got this stereotype of a man-mountain in a suit and dark glasses. But someone like that just attracts attention. Plus they tend to see physical problems with physical solutions. They'll go after the paparazzi and leave the client unprotected. Women are much better at keeping it on the down low, and using their social skills to defuse things. And a female bodyguard can blend in. That's one reason I work with so many minors. People look at me and think I'm the mom or sister or nanny. Or a friend."

A friend? Cheyenne couldn't imagine being friends with Jaydra.

"And I can sit in a restaurant or a park with a client or go shopping with them and look as if I belong."

"Do you like to go shopping?" It was hard to think of her doing something so frivolous.

Jaydra made a sound like a laugh. "Not really. Not that I could afford to shop where my clients do anyway." Her voice tightened. "Rich people think they can buy anything. Once I was the minder for this ten-year-old Middle Eastern princess visiting Manhattan. She demanded I get her a kitten, a puppy, and a baby tiger. I said I couldn't get a baby tiger, and all hell broke loose." Her voice was bitter.

"A baby tiger?"

"That's the problem with some rich people and celebrities—they're used to having things their way. They hire you for your expertise, but then they won't do what they're told. They want to stick their head up through the sunroof, or they take things from fans instead of letting you handle them first. They never think about whether it might be anthrax or a bomb."

In her mind's eye, Cheyenne saw bullets and explosions. She was finding it harder and harder to daydream about Griffin. Was she risking too much, trying to see him? "But how often does stuff like that really happen?"

"All it takes is once. But in their world, no one ever

says no to them. Well, I do. I say no. And sometimes I have to pay the price."

Cheyenne felt a twinge of guilt. Would Jaydra end up getting in trouble because of her? If she got caught, she would have to make sure her dad knew it was all her idea. "But it's impossible to keep anyone completely safe."

"You're right. But you need to choose your risks and make a plan for what to do if things go wrong. Because if you've never felt your body dump adrenaline, then when something bad happens, you'll probably just freeze. That's why I surprised you the other night, to teach you how important it is to react right away, while you still have time. Which is vital for you. You may not always be rich and famous, but you're always going to be blind."

"Yeah, I know." The words were out of her mouth before Cheyenne could call them back. "Thanks for reminding me."

Jaydra let out an irritated sigh. "All I meant is that a certain subset of people are always going to see that you're blind and think that means you'd make a great victim. But now, if you have to, you'll be able to demonstrate that's not true." She added, almost to herself, "Not that you appreciate it."

"What does that mean?"

"Because your eyes don't see, you've forgotten that you still roll them whenever you think someone's full of it.

And I've seen plenty of eye rolls from you. When I'm just trying to do my job."

Heat climbed Cheyenne's face. She hated rude people, but now it sounded like she was one. And if she rolled her eyes in front of Jaydra, who else had seen her do it? Scrambling for words, all she came up with was "I'm sorry. But you can't judge me for something I don't even know I'm doing."

"What you don't understand is I would give my life for you."

Cheyenne was finally goaded into speaking the truth. "You're just saying that. That's what you're paid to say."

"You think I'm joking?" Jaydra's voice was cold.

"Look, I appreciate it, I really do, but talking about sacrificing yourself is kind of hyperbole, isn't it? You're basically my babysitter. You're just here to make up for my dad and Danielle feeling guilty."

"This has nothing to do with Nick and Danielle. But you wouldn't understand," Jaydra said, and then stopped.

After the silence stretched on too long, Cheyenne said, "What wouldn't I understand?"

"When I was a kid, my parents were missionaries in Pakistan. There were rumors that because we were Americans, we must be rich. My little sister and I were kidnapped. Tied up, held in a hut for days. I managed to escape. She didn't."

Cheyenne knew what it was like to be tied up and

held captive. She knew what it was like to escape. But she had survived. "Wait. Do you mean your sister was, like . . ." She couldn't finish her sentence.

"Jessalyn was killed. Yes."

"How old was she?" Cheyenne asked softly.

Jaydra's voice roughened. "Just thirteen." Her tone made it clear the topic was closed. "I decided I didn't want another family to ever go through what we did."

"I'm sorry," Cheyenne said haltingly.

Instead of answering, Jaydra made a shushing sound. Cheyenne felt her straighten up.

Suddenly, the car cornered, tires squealing. Hard enough that Cheyenne's seat belt cut into her neck.

"What's the matter?" Jaydra's driving was always carefully controlled.

"Someone might be following us."

Cheyenne thought of the man snatched as he walked away from the diner, the man taken from his car before he could even retrieve the paper. Her mouth filled with bile as her lunch threatened to come back up.

They were going so fast that, even in the cocooned bubble of the car's interior, she could hear the engine revving. She pushed her feet against the floor and put her hands out to brace herself.

"Get your hands off the dash," Jaydra rapped out. "If the airbag deploys, it will break your arms."

Another hard corner, the tires chattering. The car

whined as it accelerated. What would happen next? Would their car be rammed? Would someone shoot at them? Would they spin out of control? Cheyenne pictured herself being dragged screaming from smoking wreckage.

Then unexpectedly the car began to slow.

Jaydra let out a relieved laugh. "Guess I was being paranoid. He just pulled into a driveway and got out. It was only an idiot with no idea of proper stopping distance."

CHAPTER 10

SHUT UP FOR GOOD

TJ

The present Dwayne promised TJ came the day after he visited. A portable DVD player, new in the box. Sealed, per the rules.

But thanks to Roy, who wasn't above passing off old as new, TJ knew looks could be deceiving. With plastic wrap, a hair dryer, and a little patience, you could make anything look all nice and new and shrink-wrapped.

"Too bad your friend didn't send you any DVDs to go with it," the nurse said as she handed it over. "Maybe you can borrow one from someone on the ward."

As if anyone would part with one. The rules said you couldn't have more than twelve DVDs or CDs. You couldn't have much of anything. Even if you were a bookworm or an artist, you weren't allowed more than a cubic foot of paper products.

That night TJ took the player to bed with him. Nobody

looked twice. People tended to keep a tight hold on the few things they were allowed to own. In the darkness, he fiddled with it, letting his fingers serve as his eyes. It gave him a little thrill to think that must be how Cheyenne did things.

The back was loose. With a fingernail, he unscrewed it. The insides had been gutted and replaced. He slid out what was inside and traced it with his fingers. An eight-inch pair of bolt cutters. Along with the crisp paper of a note.

Later he took it to the bathroom, read it, and then tore it in tiny pieces before flushing it away.

Meet outside of west yard fence Friday 6:15 pm.

He was going to be free. He was going to be with Cheyenne again. Eventually, he slipped into dreams of her shiny hair and soft skin.

Friday morning began with a security guard flashing the searing fluorescent lights and shouting, "Time to wake up! Rise and shine!" Then came a pleated white paper cup filled with a rainbow of pills. As he had since Dwayne's visit, TJ tucked the pills between cheek and gum. Following protocol, he opened his mouth, stuck out his tongue, and then shuffled away. The staff no longer bothered to look too closely. As Bobbi Jo, one of the nurses, had told him, "We like you, TJ. You can feed yourself, you can toilet yourself, and you never take a swing at us."

He knew what they thought. What everyone always thought. Poor old TJ. Wasn't too smart, didn't cause much trouble. Mostly did as he was told. In the bathroom, he spit the pills into the toilet, flushed, and went to breakfast.

TJ wasn't stupid, especially now he had stopped taking the pills. He was smart enough to know Oregon State Hospital wasn't really a hospital. It was a place for crazy people. Which TJ supposedly was.

He wasn't crazy, and he wasn't stupid. He was only here, in this locked ward eating cold cereal and watery juice, because of Jimbo. Back when TJ and Jimbo were working for Roy, Jimbo had liked to make fun of TJ. Called him dummy, stupid, idiot. Until finally he said things like that one too many times. So when they were hunting Cheyenne, TJ showed Jimbo who was really stupid. Stupid for calling him names when TJ had a gun in his hands.

And Jimbo had finally, *finally* shut up. TJ smiled as he took his last bite of soggy cereal. Shut up for good.

Sure, afterward he had been a little bit freaked out, TJ thought as he took his empty dishes to the conveyor belt. It was just how red everything had been, so red and shiny. He had walked away, leaving it all behind: his gun, Jimbo, and Jimbo's share of the ransom money. Money wet with Jimbo's blood. He had been a little mixed up, and by the time he remembered to look for Cheyenne, the cops had found him first.

Cheyenne. Today they would be together again. And he wouldn't let anyone or anything separate them.

Since it was a weekday, after breakfast it was time for "school" or "work." You could be a janitor, deliver mail, or work in the library, in the woodshop, or on the grounds. Patients hadn't been allowed to work in the kitchen for decades, not since one substituted poison for powdered milk and killed forty-seven residents.

A lot of the jobs were make-work, but TJ had a real job in the motor pool. After all those years taking stolen cars apart in Roy's chop shop, it was kind of nice to put them back together. He spent the day humming to himself as he rebuilt a carburetor, his mind filled with memories and daydreams of Cheyenne. When the bell rang at the end of his shift, he didn't know where the time had gone. While the supervisor counted his tools and then patted him down, TJ tried to hide his impatience. He ate only enough dinner not to get in trouble.

Cheyenne, Cheyenne, Cheyenne.

Right before yard, TJ put on his puffer jacket. The inside pocket was heavy with the bolt cutter. As he pulled a plastic chair up to the fence, he looked around. Two employees sat at a picnic table, talking. Another surreptitiously checked his phone. A couple of others scanned the grounds, but by their posture, he could tell they expected to see nothing out of the ordinary. It was a warm day filled with birds chirping, the low hum of insects, the murmur of the nearby freeway.

Like he always did now, TJ linked his left hand in the fence. His right hand looked like it was doing the same, but really he was biting at the wire with the bolt cutter hidden in his curled fingers. His hands were strong. Snip, snip, snip. Until finally he made a hole just big enough for him. A TJ-sized hole.

And then, when no one was looking, he slipped through.

CHAPTER 11

ANY STRANGER

CHEYENNE

Several hours after Jaydra thought they were being followed, Cheyenne still felt shaky. Jaydra had said a black SUV had swung in behind them, so close she couldn't even see the license plate. The driver, a man wearing sunglasses, had followed them around the first hard corner—but then pulled into a driveway.

As soon as they got home, Cheyenne had gone to her room and locked her door. She wasn't in the mood for Jaydra deciding to spring something on her.

Now she lay stretched out on her bed, listening to music, writing and rewriting a message to Griffin about Monday. What would happen when they were finally together again? That thought made her shaky too, but in a different way. What would they talk about? Should she hug him right away? What should she wear? If she put on more makeup than normal or wore perfume, would Jaydra get suspicious?

When her phone said, "Text from Dad," she jumped.

"Cheyenne, could you please come out to the patio?"

She froze. She hadn't even realized her dad was home. She had thought he was still in Tokyo or Amsterdam or someplace. But he was clearly here, and now he wanted to talk to her. Had the school realized they hadn't badged out for lunch? Or could he have found her Facebook page? Even—her stomach rose—discovered her plan to ditch school Monday to see Griffin?

Telling herself she was being paranoid, Cheyenne texted back. "What's up?"

"Just come."

Phantom jumped off the bed when she got up, but she told him to stay. She didn't work him at home. Even a guide dog needed times to just be a dog. Besides, Cheyenne knew how many steps it was to each room, knew the location of every piece of furniture. The knowledge ran like her own personal GPS in the background of her thoughts, telling her when to swivel her hips past the sculpture in the living room or when to reach for a doorknob. And since the accident three years ago, she had learned the hard way—they all had—how important it was to keep everything tidy. No more clothes scattered on her bedroom floor or boxes set down in the entryway.

Since she was going outside, she grabbed the new cane Jaydra had gotten for her. It was made of the same kind of aluminum they used in planes, and it folded down to nearly nothing. She shook it out, enjoying the sound of all the parts snapping together as the rope inside went taut.

After the air-conditioned chill of the house, the sun felt good on her skin. Cheyenne never used to pay attention to the sun, or whether she was facing east or west. One of the first things the orientation and mobility instructor had taught her was to always orient herself using cardinal directions.

"We're over here," her dad called. The sweet scent of roses filled her nostrils. Bees hummed, and in the distance, the neighbor's sprinkler pattered. Without her eyes, her other senses had come alive. In some ways, sighted people were just as handicapped as she was, although they wouldn't believe it if she told them.

Her cane found one of the Adirondack chairs. She nudged it with her knee, making sure it was unoccupied. A few times she had sat on someone when she mistakenly thought a seat was empty.

"So what's up?" She shivered, suddenly chilled. The sun must have gone behind a cloud. When Duke butted her knees, she scratched him behind the ears, grateful for the distraction. He leaned into her with a happy groan.

"We have a surprise for you," Danielle said. "Actually, two surprises."

"Let's focus on this one for now, honey," Nick said. Some kind of emotion edged his voice. And he never called either of them pet names.

"What kind of surprise?" Maybe it was for her birthday next week.

"There's going to be some changes this next year," Danielle said.

"Are you going back to work?" Since Danielle was already volunteering several shifts a week at a clinic for low-income patients, it seemed a likely next step.

"Not exactly."

Cheyenne wanted to scream. Why couldn't they just spit it out? "Then what?"

"We're expecting," Danielle said. Her laugh was giddy.

But Danielle was old! She was thirty-nine. Too old to have a baby. Only evidently not.

Finally Cheyenne managed to say, "That's great!" She heard them kiss. Just because she couldn't see it didn't mean that hearing it was okay. She held herself very still. Tried to make her face smile. Hoped they couldn't read her as well as Jaydra could.

"We waited to tell you until the first trimester was over," Danielle finally said, "but it's getting to the point I can't hide it anymore."

Their family wasn't much on full-body hugs. Thinking back over the last few months, Cheyenne remembered a few times conversations had seemed to switch tracks when she came into the room. But it hurt that they had kept it a secret from her when it sounded like any stranger could just glance over and see the truth. Jaydra certainly had to know.

The silence stretched out. Cheyenne knew she had to say something more. *First trimester.* "So you're, like, twelve weeks pregnant?"

"Due right before Christmas. And"—Danielle's voice rose with excitement—"it's a girl!"

"After the baby's born," Nick said, "I'm not going to be traveling as often. Dani made me promise." He patted Cheyenne's knee. "I know I wasn't around as much as I should have been when you were a kid. Now I want to get it right."

When Cheyenne was growing up, her dad had been gone so much that her mom was basically a single mom, only with more money. It was her mom who had known her best, who knew everything about her. She was the only person who shared most of Cheyenne's memories of birthdays and holidays and heartbreaks.

Those first few terrible months after the car accident, her dad had cut back on traveling, hiring nurses to fill in the gaps, including Danielle. She was the one who finally forced Cheyenne to get out of the bed she refused to leave long after her broken bones had healed. It was Danielle who cajoled and goaded Cheyenne to find a way to resume life. And somewhere along the way, her dad had fallen in love with her.

Cheyenne genuinely liked her stepmom, but she would never call her Mom. Never betray her own mom like that. Besides, Danielle hadn't tried to take over that role. Now it seemed she wouldn't need to, because she would have her own child. A child who could see.

Jealousy stabbed Cheyenne, followed quickly by shame. Why couldn't she be happy for them?

"Are you okay?" her dad asked.

"I miss Mom," she choked out, picking the least complicated emotion she was feeling. Her mother was the last person she had seen, would ever see. Cheyenne had turned to her a split second before the car hit them. The headlights silhouetted her short, dark, curly hair, outlined her mouth opening in surprise. And then everything had gone black.

Cheyenne had been able to tell her mom anything. Of course that was three years ago, when she was thirteen, just a kid. If her mom were alive now, would it be the same?

To hide her tears, she leaned down and nuzzled Duke's neck, knowing she wasn't fooling anyone. Least of all herself. Even Duke pulled away.

Danielle whispered something to her dad. Then in a louder voice she said, "I'm going to get the hose. Those roses are starting to look droopy."

Desperate to change the subject, Cheyenne asked, "Where's Octavio?" He had been their gardener for years, but for the past two days, whenever she had taken Phantom out to do his business, Octavio hadn't called out a greeting the way he normally did. He was one of the few men besides her dad that Duke tolerated. When she talked to him, Cheyenne could still picture his wide smile, framed by his carefully maintained narrow mustache. When she was little, the thin dark lines of hair that bracketed his mouth and went all the way to his chin had reminded her of a puppet.

"He must be sick." As Danielle spoke, her voice went farther away. "His phone just goes to voice mail." Cheyenne heard the hose being pulled through the grass and then water splashing.

Her dad got up and settled on the arm of her chair. "Are you okay?"

"It was just a surprise, that's all. I'm really glad for you." She put a smile on her face, wondering how deep he could see inside her. She didn't think she could handle being out here for another minute. Abruptly, she stood. "I've got a ton of homework I have to do this weekend. I'd better get started."

"Cheyenne—" Her dad put a hand on her arm, but she shook it off.

"Don't worry, I'm fine. And I *am* happy for you."

She managed to hold off her tears until she was inside.

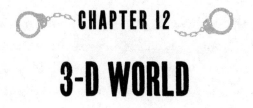

CHAPTER 12

3-D WORLD

CHEYENNE

Cheyenne closed the door to her room, threw herself on her bed, and buried her face in her cool pillow.

Her dad and Danielle were having a baby. She was going to have a little sister. She should be happy. Right?

But it was like one of those fairy tales where you got three wishes, and instead of endless riches, you ended up with a sausage stuck to your nose. How many times before the accident had Cheyenne begged her parents for a baby brother or sister? Instead she had gotten a dog. And Spencer had died in the same accident that killed her mom and took Cheyenne's sight.

Now, ten years too late, she *was* getting a little sister, only it wasn't anything like she had imagined. Grief for her mom and envy of the sister she didn't even have yet crested over Cheyenne like a wave, threatening to drown her. If her mom were here, she could pour out all the knotted, ugly emotions that crowded her thoughts and roiled her belly.

To Cheyenne's embarrassment, her mom had talked to perfect strangers as if they were friends, and sometimes they really became her friends. While Danielle was always quiet and self-contained, her mom had been loud and funny.

The same things that mortified Cheyenne at thirteen were the traits she now desperately missed. Her mom would have understood how she could be jealous and sad over good news. Still, she felt ashamed. How could she be angry about a baby? Babies were innocent.

If her mom were here now, she would listen without judging or offering solutions. And then she would tell Cheyenne it would all be okay. And somehow, maybe because it was her mom, Cheyenne would believe it.

Whining low in his throat, Phantom stood pressed against the bed. Finally, Cheyenne put out her hand to stroke his head. Phantom's ears were pinned back. He nosed her hand anxiously. When she patted the space next to her, he scrambled up, crawled forward, and licked her face. Wiping her tears on his rough fur, she took a deep shuddery breath.

It was just that her dad had sounded so happy when he talked about the baby. When was the last time he had sounded like that talking about Cheyenne?

Would he end up loving her sister more? He had to

look at Cheyenne and wonder what would happen to her, the same way she wondered herself. She planned to go to a local college, but how would she ever get a job? Would she be able to make enough money to support herself? Would she just have to live at home forever?

Even though babies cried and pooped and needed constant care, everyone still thought they were adorable. Part of it was the way they looked: big eyes, button noses, rosebud mouths. Except Cheyenne would never be able to see those things.

People also loved babies because they knew they would grow and change, that their helpless stage was only temporary. But even though her dad had sent Cheyenne to the best doctors, none of them offered hope that she would regain her sight. And once people realized she was blind, they often treated her like she was still a child. Or, worse, like she was mentally handicapped.

She would love the baby, of course she would. But her sister would see all the things Cheyenne would never see again. Their dad and Danielle, as well as the faces of a thousand other people. Phantom and Duke. The Degas lithograph of a dancer that still hung on her wall, even though she hadn't seen it for nearly four years. Her sister would be able to look out Cheyenne's window and see flowers, birds, clouds scudding across the sky. The whole 3-D world.

Cheyenne had stopped crying, but her breath was still coming in hitches.

Her Facebook account chimed with a message. It was from Griffin.

"Haven't heard from you all day. Is everything okay?"

"Yes," she lied. The news about the baby was still too raw to share. "Sorry. In fact, I have something to tell you."

"I have something to tell you, too. It's that I can't stop thinking about you."

Heat climbed her face. "Me too." Her heart was beating so fast. "I mean, I can't stop thinking about you."

"I want to see you so bad."

If she went to Griffin on Monday, she wouldn't see him, or at least not more than a blurry slice. But she would hear him, smell him. Touch him. Maybe even taste him.

"I figured out how to see you Monday," she typed. "I can sneak out of school, and my friend can take me to you." She could feel her heartbeat in her ears, her throat, her fingertips.

"But Monday's forever. I want to see you now."

Cheyenne shook her head as if they were already in the same room together. "I can't. It's not possible. Anytime I'm out of the house and not at school, Jaydra's always with me."

"But we're only a few miles apart," Griffin typed. "If you could just get out to the street, I could pick you up."

"Where would you get a car?"

"My aunt's renting one, and I can borrow it."

Weren't there rules about who could drive a rental car?

Cheyenne had a feeling it didn't include seventeen-year-olds. "Wouldn't you get in trouble?"

"I could explain it to her later."

She bit her lip. She was so tempted. If she said yes, she might be with him in an hour or two. But then reality prevailed.

"There's no way I could leave without getting in a lot of trouble." Not with just her dad and Danielle, but maybe with the prosecutor as well. "But on Monday, I should be able to leave school without anyone knowing."

Griffin kept asking, and she kept saying no.

But still part of Cheyenne said, what did it matter if she took off now?

CHAPTER 13

JUST DO IT

CHEYENNE

It was nearly ten when Cheyenne woke up. She and Griffin had messaged back and forth until well after midnight. When she finally slept, her dreams had been filled with a confusing jumble of Griffin, the baby, her mom, and memories of what had happened six months earlier. Even after taking a shower, she wasn't fully awake.

As she walked down the hall toward the kitchen, she heard a stranger's voice speaking to her dad and Danielle.

She slowed her steps. But her dad must have heard her, because he called out, "Hey, Cheyenne, could you come to the living room?"

Combing her fingers through her still-wet hair, she complied, wondering who it was.

When she felt her feet step on the soft oriental rug, she stopped.

"Cheyenne," her dad said, "I'd like you to meet Ronald Winston."

"Hello." She wondered who he was. Hopefully not some new layer of security.

"Remember when we said yesterday that there were two surprises?" Danielle said brightly. "This is the second."

"What is?" Cheyenne felt itchy waiting for whatever was to come.

"I know you haven't been looking forward to the trial next week," her dad said, "and I'm sorry you've been having to go through all this, especially right before your birthday."

"It's nobody's fault."

He cleared his throat. "Anyway, we have a little surprise for you. That's where Ronald comes in. He's one of the lead engineers for the project."

Cheyenne still wasn't following. "What project?"

"A self-driving car," Ronald answered.

"I've already put an order in for you," her dad added, "but the car won't be in production for a while yet. So we worked out a deal for you to have a prototype on loan for the weekend."

"Self-driving?" Cheyenne echoed. "Wait—you mean it's a car I could drive by myself?"

"Well, it's actually the car that drives itself," Ronald

said. "And since it's a prototype, I'll be in the passenger seat at all times."

Danielle added, "And your dad or Jaydra or I will be in the backseat."

It was almost too much to take in. First the baby and now this. "Is it really safe to have *me* in the driver's seat?" It had taken her a long time to trust that Phantom wouldn't walk under a branch or a sign that would hit her head. It had been days before she stopped flinching, imagining she could feel something looming a few inches ahead, ready to slam into her face. How much harder would it be to trust a car?

Ronald cleared his throat. "Our cars are actually much better drivers than people with twenty-twenty vision. This car looks everyplace at once and never gets distracted. It can track other vehicles, bicyclists, and pedestrians as far away as two football fields."

"How can it do all that stuff?" Cheyenne still felt skeptical.

"Let's go outside and take a look at it," Ronald said, and then stammered, "I mean, um, examine it."

"It's okay." Cheyenne was used to people tying themselves into verbal knots around her. "You can say words like *see* or *look* around me. I say them all the time. It doesn't bother me."

As they walked outside, Cheyenne lightly rested her

hand on her dad's arm. "This doesn't feel real. Maybe I'm still dreaming."

"Well, it's two big things in two days," he said. "And they've both been in the works for a while." He came to a stop in the driveway.

"This car has features that a lot of other cars already have, but it uses them in smarter ways," Ronald said. His tone reminded her of Jaydra, of how she loved to explain things. "It's got GPS, but that's too static to use by itself. A lot of cars have backup cameras, but this car has cameras on all sides. And it's got radar so it can see in rain or snow or when it's dark. Even that's not new. Most higher-end cars now have radar as part of adaptive cruise control. The only part that's really new is the lasers on top of the car."

"It looks like a yellow spinning siren light." Her dad lifted Cheyenne's hand to the top of the car so she could feel it.

"Those lasers give the car a three-dimensional view, while a human driver can look in only one direction at a time," Ronald said. "The car takes all these pieces of information and turns them into things like steering, speeding up, or stopping. In another ten years, it will be talking to all the other cars around it. That will actually make things a lot easier."

"Because it's drivers, not cars, that make mistakes," Danielle said.

"Your mom's right. Drivers get drunk, fall asleep, overcorrect, speed. Basically, people, being people, tend to do stupid things. I've spent a lot of time in our prototypes. You see people weaving because they're texting, or reading, or holding a quart of ice cream in one hand and a spoon in the other. Once I even saw a guy playing a trumpet."

Cheyenne found the flaw in his argument for the car's perfection. "But even if this car drives perfectly, what about other drivers?"

"We've programmed the car so it knows that people aren't always logical, that they might signal left and go right, or put their signal on and keep going straight. That's why it knows to wait a second after a light turns green, in case people aren't paying attention or decide to run the light."

It still felt like there had to be a catch. "Is it legal for me to drive it?"

"As long as you have a licensed driver sitting next to you who could take control in an emergency," Ronald said. "That's why I'll be there. It's the same as it would be for a fifteen-year-old with a learner's permit."

"We're going to try to get the law fine-tuned so that you can just drive it yourself," her dad added.

Cheyenne didn't doubt that he would make it happen. Nike was one of Oregon's most important companies, and whatever her dad wanted tended to happen.

It would be so wonderful to go someplace by herself.

To not be dependent on anyone. She imagined rolling down the window and feeling the wind in her hair. She could take off for Seattle. Or drive to the ocean, sit on the sand, and let Phantom chase the waves.

"Want to give it a try?" Ronald said.

"What, right now?"

"No time like the present," her dad said, then repeated the old Nike slogan. "Just do it." She heard him open the car door.

Cheyenne stepped forward, found the seat, sat down, and swung in her legs. She took a deep breath of new car smell. In front of her was a steering wheel. On the floor, her feet nudged two pedals.

Behind her she heard her dad and Danielle climbing in, while Ronald took the seat next to her.

"Buckle up," he said.

Was this really happening?

"Now you're going to start the car," Ronald said.

She swept her fingers around the dash and steering wheel, but found nothing but buttons and dials. "Where's the key?"

"There isn't any actual key, not anymore. There's just a fob you have to have inside the car, like in your pocket or purse. I have it on me. And the start button is on the dashboard at about your four o'clock."

She grazed her fingers over the dash until she found it. It was round, about the size of a half-dollar.

"Now put your foot on the brake, which is the floor pedal farthest to the left, and then press the start button."

"If this is a self-driving car, why does it have a brake and a steering wheel?"

Ronald sighed. "We've had to add a number of redundant safety features in this introductory phase. They're not really necessary, but they make lawmakers more willing to change the rules. So you have a brake pedal, I have a brake pedal, and there's also an emergency stop button on the center console that anyone in the car can reach. I could also stop the car with my laptop."

"Can you drive it with your laptop?"

"Not remotely, at least not right now. Either the car drives itself or, in some kind of emergency, the driver uses the steering wheel. So go ahead, put your foot on the brake and start the car."

Cheyenne's palms were sweaty. Even if the car was supposed to do all the thinking and make all the decisions, even if Ronald was right here beside her, what if she did something wrong and got them all—including the baby inside Danielle—killed?

She pressed the button and was answered with a soft hum.

"Now you just need to tell it where to go," Ronald said.

"Where should I say?"

"How about your school?" Danielle suggested.

"The pane for navigation is in the middle of the dash," Ronald said. "There, that's it, the top one. Now press that small button on the top left, say where you want to go, and press it again."

She followed his instructions, overenunciating her words. "Catlin Gabel."

"Catlin Gabel is located at 8825 Southwest Barnes Road. Is that correct?" It was a woman's voice, not that much different from the one on her computer, only not as fast.

"Yes."

"Developing navigation route. There are three choices. One avoids the freeway. Do you wish to avoid the freeway?"

Cheyenne waited for Ronald to give her some hint as to what to answer, but he was silent. Finally she said, "Yes." She wanted to say more than these simple one-word answers. She wanted to ask Ronald a question. But she worried the navigation system was still listening to her and would be confused by whatever she said.

"Will it hear me?" she whispered.

"Not if you're the one initiating the conversation and you don't press the button. It will consult with you, and that's the point where you need to be careful to not have too much background noise or other conversations, or it might need to ask for clarification."

"Auto driving," the computer said.

Cheyenne's stomach lurched as she felt the car begin to move.

CHAPTER 14

STRANGERS' BONES

GRIFFIN

Griffin took a sip of weak coffee, which he had watered down even further with milk. His stomach was churning. He and Aunt Debby were having lunch at a small café, which was crowded on a Saturday. He'd managed to swallow two bites of his cheese sandwich, but then had to put it down. Later in the afternoon, what remained of his mom would be returned to the earth. Only this time there would be a stone to mark where she lay.

Aunt Debby broke the silence between them. "You've got some crumbs here." She mimed brushing her chest.

He busied himself, first with the flat of his hand, then with licked fingers to pick up a few stragglers from the crisp shirt.

He hadn't noticed it so much back in Chicago, when they were surrounded by her family, but the longer Griffin was with Debby in Portland, the more she reminded him of his mom. It wasn't any one thing, but a million small ones. The way she held her shoulders, the turns of phrase she used, the emotions she didn't express but showed in fleeting expressions.

While he waited for her to finish her soup, he took out a pen and began to sketch on a napkin. He drew a tree standing alone on a barren stretch of land. Not only was it bare of leaves, but all the limbs ended abruptly, as if they had been pruned too far back. Debby watched as he shaded the underside of a branch, and then she said it was time to go. As they got up, she squeezed his hand. He left the napkin crumpled on the table.

On the drive to the cemetery, they didn't speak. Aunt Debby kept one hand on the wheel, the fingers of her other hand twisting in her hair. The sky matched Griffin's mood. It was the color of cement, shading to charcoal in the west. The air felt heavy, like a storm was coming.

They parked and then walked over the grass to the spot where the coffin was waiting. Not wanting to walk over strangers' bones, Griffin zigzagged between the graves. Aunt Debby plowed straight ahead.

Ahead of them, the turf had been cut away and lay to one side in a neat stack of narrow strips. The newly turned earth smelled fresh and clean. A piece of bright green Astroturf with a rectangle in the middle had been laid over the grave itself.

Above the expanse of fake green, his mother's coffin

hung suspended, resting on canvas webbing slung between two sets of silver poles. Brown and high-domed, the coffin was so shiny that Griffin wondered if it was really wood. If he could look inside, what would he see? Had they bothered to rearrange her bones the way an archeologist might after a dig, or simply tossed them in? The two bites of sandwich threatened to come back up.

A man in a polyester suit gave them a tight smile and a nod. He was wearing a name tag, so Griffin figured he was from the funeral home.

He wondered if the canvas ever tore, the poles ever slipped, the coffin went tumbling? It was all just covering up where his mom was going to go, a big hole in the earth, just like the hole out in the back pasture Roy had dug for her years ago with the Cat.

In the next fifteen minutes, they were joined by a scattering of what he was told were old neighbors and people who remembered his mom from part-time jobs she'd had. Debby introduced him to each one, and each time Griffin promptly forgot their name and connection to his mom. He couldn't focus on anything.

Finally the priest showed up. He was wheezing before he even reached the grave, his face red. The two dozen people listened—or pretended to—as he greeted them and then began to drone on from something in the Bible.

Griffin's neck itched. The scar was made of thinner, more fragile skin. Not tough like you would think a scar would be. He loosened his tie, but it still felt like it was rubbing his skin raw.

The priest just seemed to be going through the motions. He didn't meet anyone's eyes, and his voice was a low mumble. Griffin shifted from foot to foot in his shiny dress shoes. It was all he could do not to break into a run.

Finally it was over. Griffin walked off. Debby barely noticed him go. She was talking to that old lady, the one who used to go to church with his mom. He waited until he was a couple of hundred feet away and Aunt Debby had her back turned before he pulled out a cigarette.

Mom was really gone. Griffin had always imagined that she was in Chicago, eating deep-dish pizza. Maybe listening to jazz, which was about the only other thing he had associated with Chicago at the time. Not thinking about him, obviously, because she never called, never sent a birthday card or even an e-mail.

He had thought she was probably remarried, with a new family. That she had a better husband, one who didn't fight with her. One who had a regular job. And a kid who wasn't scarred. Who could read without stumbling.

Tears pricked Griffin's eyes, and he angrily blinked them away. He wasn't a little kid anymore. He didn't need a mom.

CHAPTER 15

HERE AND GONE

CHEYENNE

That evening, Cheyenne couldn't wipe the grin from her face. Today had been amazing. With her sitting in the driver's seat, she had "driven" Ronald, Danielle, and her dad to school and back. After lunch, Jaydra and Phantom had gotten in the backseat, and they had gone to Phantom's favorite dog park. The three of them had taken turns throwing a tennis ball until Phantom was too exhausted to chase it anymore.

Afterward, they had gone out for ice cream. Jaydra had made Cheyenne wait at an outside table wearing a baseball cap and sunglasses, but still it had been great to be someplace that wasn't home or school. It didn't matter that while eating her hot fudge sundae she had to listen to Jaydra and Ronald discuss boring technical aspects of the car. It didn't even matter when some creepy guy recognized her and Jaydra decided they had to get back in the car and go. The weird thing about the car was that Cheyenne could keep eating even when she was in the driver's seat.

Now Cheyenne lay on her bed and logged on to Facebook, ready to tell Griffin all about it. But a series of messages was already waiting for her.

When she heard her computer read them, the smile left her face.

"Went to Mom's service today. Old man saying words over a hole in the ground. He never even knew her. She was here and gone and for what?"

Followed an hour later by "Cheyenne, are you there?"

Then "Cheyenne, please I need to talk to you."

And finally "Cheyenne, please."

The last message had been left over an hour ago. Her stomach twisted. "Griffin, are you okay?" she wrote back. But his messages hadn't sounded okay. They hadn't sounded okay at all.

For nearly thirty minutes she waited, chewing on a thumbnail. From the living room came the faint sounds of her dad and Danielle laughing with Ronald and Jaydra. The happy sounds grated on her.

Finally her computer chimed with an incoming message. She slipped her headphones back on as her finger flew to tap the button to play it.

"I can't take this anymore, Cheyenne. I need to see you so bad."

"It's just two more days."

"The prosecutor scheduled another meeting Monday. That means I won't be able to see you. But, Cheyenne, I have to. I need to. Please. Tell them you're going for a walk and take Phantom. I could meet you in that park down the street."

If he knew about the park, he must have already managed to drive by her house. "Do you have your aunt's car?"

"No. I just took off. Left Aunt Debby and everything. I'll figure out a way to get there. I need to see you. You're like the only good thing left in this world."

"There's just no way I can leave now, Griffin. But the prosecutor can't meet with you all day Monday. As soon as you're free, I'll come to you."

"Monday's too late. I don't think I'll be here then."

Everything stilled. What did he mean? "Are you leaving?"

"That's one way to put it."

The ice cream she had eaten earlier felt like it was alive and squirming in her gut. "Griffin—are you talking about hurting yourself?"

"I can't testify against my own dad. I'm not sure I can do this anymore, Cheyenne."

With shaking fingers, she typed, "Can't do what?"

"This. Life."

"Don't say that." But part of Cheyenne understood. After the accident, after her mom died, she wanted to die, too. Life seemed random and terrible. Why should you bother to love or even care about anything, when it all could be taken away in a second?

"No matter what happens, remember me."

"Don't say things like that." She wished she could type even faster. "Tell me where you are. I can come to you."

"You already said that there's no way."

"There is a way." If there wasn't, she would make one. "I know you never meant to take me. I won't let you hurt yourself over something that was an accident." She took a shaky breath and then added, "Just tell me where you are and promise you'll wait for me."

If she did what she was thinking of doing, her dad and Danielle and Jaydra would kill her. Not to mention Ronald.

But if she didn't do it, Griffin might kill himself.

CHAPTER 16

YOU KNOW WHAT TO DO

CHEYENNE

Cheyenne waited until everyone was in bed and the house was quiet. Because Jaydra was living in the guesthouse, Ronald was staying in the extra bedroom, which was one door down from Cheyenne's. On the other side of his room was the gym. Then came the bulk of the house: the kitchen, the dining nook, the formal dining room, and the living room. On the far side was another hall with her dad and Danielle's room as well as an office and a library. Which room, she wondered briefly as she tried to make a plan to get away, would be turned into the baby's?

The self-driving car was outside in the circular driveway. When the gates sensed the weight of a vehicle leaving, they would open automatically. She could tell the car's computer where Griffin was: a country road not far from where his mother had been buried. And then it would take her to him.

All she needed was the key—or the key fob—to make the car start. Only where was it?

Just before midnight, she slowly opened the door to the hall and began to make her way toward the kitchen, avoiding every floorboard that creaked. Outside, it had started to rain, which provided her with a little bit of cover. Phantom padded beside her, hoping for a meal or at least a treat. Afraid that he would whine, she didn't try to make him stay in her room.

Once Cheyenne was in the kitchen, she ran her hands over the spot on the counter where they kept keys and charged phones and her dad put his wallet when he was home. She found all of those, but not the fob Ronald had told her about earlier. It had probably never left the pocket of his pants.

His pants, which must now be in the guest room. Was it possible to creep in while he was sleeping? She knew the layout of the room, but she would have to explore to find the fob. She missed being able to look into a room and know immediately what was in it. And no matter how quiet she was, chances were good that he would wake up and then she would have some big-time explaining to do. Claiming to be sleepwalking probably wouldn't cut it.

Could she risk waiting until morning, when Ronald would be taking a shower, and she might be able to sneak into his room? But then how would she make it to the car without being caught? Both Danielle and Nick were early risers. And Cheyenne needed a head start before they figured out what was happening.

Phantom scraped his bowl across the floor, reminding her that he was hungry, or at least wanted to eat. She peeled back the lid on a can of dog food and shook it until it slid into the bowl. While he gulped it down, her thoughts chased themselves. She had promised that she would go to Griffin as soon as she could. If she took too long, would his dark thoughts overwhelm him?

Since she couldn't get into Ronald's room, she had to get him out. Every bedroom had its own bathroom, so it wasn't like she could wait and hope that he might pad down the hall in his PJs to answer nature's call. No, she had to roust him.

But first she had to deal with Phantom. She didn't need him following her, giving her away. It sounded like he had wolfed down most of his food. She unlocked the back door and pushed him outside into the light rain, hoping he wouldn't whine. Duke's doghouse wasn't big enough for two.

In the kitchen cupboard, she found the bags of popcorn and took one to the microwave. Each button had a series of Braille dots Danielle had made with a labeler. Popcorn took ninety seconds. Cheyenne put in the bag, closed the door, and set it for nine minutes.

Then she slipped inside the hall closet across from Ronald's room and waited. She kept the door open a crack, pressing her left eye against it. By her watch, it took five minutes for the smoke alarm to go off. Which was at least two minutes after her nose had started picking up the stench.

A few seconds after the alarm started to blare, she heard Ronald's door fly open and saw a shadow cross her vision. His footsteps pounded toward the front door. A second later, she darted across the hall and into his room, closing the door behind her. Her outstretched hands were already running across the bureau while one foot nudged the floor for his suitcase.

On the other side of the house, Nick and Danielle were shouting her name. Outside, Phantom and Duke had started to bark.

Ronald had draped his pants over the back of a chair, and the second Cheyenne lifted them, she felt the weight of the fob. She fumbled it out. It was heavy and rectangular, with rounded edges. She slipped it into her pocket and darted back into the hall. As soon as she opened the door, acrid smoke stung her eyes and nose.

Her dad yelled for her again. He sounded close. She hoped he hadn't seen her leave Ronald's room. A second later, Danielle grabbed her arm.

"Oh my God, Cheyenne, I was so worried."

"We need to get out of the house right now," her dad said. "There's a fire."

Cheyenne didn't have to fake the anxiety in her voice. "I must have pressed the wrong button on the microwave before I went to the bathroom. Sorry, sorry, this is all my fault."

Behind Danielle, Jaydra said, "The popcorn caught on fire, but it was contained within the microwave. We'll need to open all the windows and doors to clear the smoke, and turn on the kitchen exhaust fan, but everything's fine. Except for the microwave. That's ruined."

"I don't care about the microwave." Danielle's voice had an edge of hysteria. "I was only worried about Cheyenne." She pulled her into a hug. Cheyenne moved to one side so her stepmom didn't notice the lump of the fob in her right-hand pocket. She bumped into Danielle's wet cheek and then the rounded bulge of her belly. The first made her feel guilty. The second made her feel things she couldn't name.

In the kitchen, the alarm finally stopped. Outside she heard her dad trying to calm the dogs while he talked to Ronald.

"What's weird is that when I came out, I found Phantom in the yard," Jaydra said. Was there suspicion in her voice?

"I let him out before I put the popcorn in. And then

I went to the bathroom." Cheyenne realized they might be wondering why she was still dressed. "I was just so excited about today that I couldn't sleep."

"And you rushed out of the bathroom when you heard the smoke alarm?" Jaydra asked.

Cheyenne had to swallow before she answered. If they noticed, she hoped they just chalked it up to the smoke in the air. "Yeah. I'm really, really sorry."

"That's not why I'm asking. I just want to make sure you know what to do in a fire. If you think there's a fire or you hear an alarm, never open the door until you know it's safe. If you feel heat or smoke coming through the cracks, don't open it. Same goes if the door is hot or the knob is. That's when you might have to go out a window. And if there's smoke, get low and crawl on your hands and knees."

Cheyenne nodded like a robot.

The adults busied themselves opening windows, letting in clean rain-scented air. Her dad carried the ruined microwave outside, while Cheyenne toweled off Phantom's fur. Eventually everyone went back to bed.

She waited a full hour before she risked leaving, messaging Griffin that she was almost on her way. He asked her to hurry, which made her palms sweat even more. She pushed her folded cane into the pocket of her raincoat. Phantom tried to follow her out, but she made him stay inside her room. She was already nervous enough about driving the car, and she didn't want to have to divide her attention. Luckily, he didn't protest. He was probably too tired from all the excitement of the day. With the fob heavy in her hand, she ghosted down the hallway.

When she opened the back door, a bark greeted her. Uh-oh. She had forgotten about Duke. He was still agitated from the commotion.

She urgently whispered, "Leave it!," the all-purpose instruction to tell him to stop doing whatever he was doing, but Duke just barked again. When she opened the car door, he crowded in past her.

She could try to wrestle him out, but Cheyenne's skin was itching as if Jaydra already had eyes on her. So instead she just climbed in, shoving Duke over to the passenger seat. The car fob went into a cup holder. She put her foot on the brake and pressed the button. And then she told the car where to go.

CHAPTER 17

IMPOSSIBLE

CHEYENNE

The car hummed quietly. Sitting behind the wheel, Cheyenne pictured how she was speeding through the darkness with Duke by her side. At first they had been on the smooth freeway, where she had occasionally caught flashes of the lights of passing cars. Now the road was rougher. All she could see out of the corner of her left eye was blackness. Even though Ronald had said the car had over ten thousand miles on it, it still had that new-car smell, mingled now with the scents of damp dog.

Lightly, Cheyenne rested her hands on the steering wheel, felt it spin under her sweaty palms.

Then she pulled them away. What if something she did prompted the car to switch to manual mode? What if she couldn't get it going again? It had been one thing when Ronald was sitting next to her, but now she would have to figure everything out on her own. It was oddly comforting having Duke beside her. She just hoped that he would react well to Griffin. Even though it had been Griffin's dad, not Griffin, who beat him, the association wouldn't help, and he didn't like men in general.

The address Griffin had given her was south of the Portland city limits, on a road she had never heard of. Silently, she urged the car to go faster. She wondered if that was even possible. The engineers probably hadn't programmed it to speed.

Finally, after a series of turns, the car began to slow. "Destination reached," the computerized voice said. "Auto parking." It nosed to what must have been the side of the road.

Taking a deep breath, Cheyenne opened the car door. She got out, Duke crowding her heels. Her legs were shaking. Gravel crunched under her feet. Otherwise it was quiet. She listened for Griffin's voice but heard nothing.

"Griffin? Griffin?" Her voice sounded like it was falling into a void.

No answer.

As Duke pressed close against her legs, she swiveled her head, but it was too dark for her slice of vision to show anything. She strained to hear a voice or footsteps or anything besides herself and Duke. A faint breeze caressed her cheek, rustling whatever grew in the fields around her. The breeze created the field for her. She sniffed, but could smell nothing but the fresh scent of recently fallen rain and the smoke that still clung to her skin. In the distance, the low hum of a car faded even as she tuned in to it.

Otherwise, it was absolutely still.

"Griffin?" she called again.

A chill ran over her skin, and she shivered. Was she too late? Had Griffin made good on his hints? The thought froze her heart.

Or had he gotten tired of waiting for her and gone someplace else? She thought about pulling out her cane and setting off to look for him. But where would she go? She had no mental map of this place.

"Griffin?" she called again, then held her breath.

Silence. It seemed like she was alone, except for Duke, who let out a low whine.

But was she really alone? Apart from the breeze, did she hear a soft sound? At first she thought it came from her left, but then she sensed it on the right.

Were her senses playing tricks on her, or was someone nearby? With a prickle, the hair rose on the back of her neck.

"I can hear you," she said definitely, although she still wasn't certain. "Who's there? Is that you, Griffin?"

Beside her, Duke's whine shifted to a whimper. Cheyenne put her hand over his snout. "Leave it!" she whispered, and was shocked when he nipped. Maybe he sensed Griffin and was afraid of him. Duke had only known Griffin from before, when Roy was beating both of them. When they were under the sway of a bad man.

A voice came from ahead of her, on her left. "TJ's right. You are a pretty little thing."

Cheyenne let out a shriek. The man sounded like Roy. But that was impossible. Roy was in jail. Her thoughts were a crazy scramble as she whirled around, pulled open the car door, and tried to dive inside.

But Duke was right beside her with the same panicked plan. His claws dug into her leg as he frantically pushed ahead of her. She ducked her head inside the door. Duke's tail slapped her face when he turned around, barking so loudly it hurt her ears. She grabbed the steering wheel and dragged her torso inside, then pulled both her legs in.

But before Cheyenne could close the door, a hand clamped on her left wrist and began to pull her out. Duke growled and snapped, his jaws inches from her face, his nails digging painfully into her thighs.

She twisted her wrist toward her attacker's thumb—the weakest part of the grip. Bracing her feet on the floor, she let go of the steering wheel and grabbed the door handle with her right hand. She managed to yank her left hand free at the same time as she tried to pull the door closed. But instead of hearing the door latch into place, she felt the window part of the door close on the man's hand.

He screamed a swear word in her ear and then fell

back into the gravel as she slammed the door closed. With her left hand, she skimmed the door, trying to find the button or switch to lock it. At the same time, she reached over Duke with her right hand and pushed the start button. Nothing.

Her heart felt like it would beat out of her chest. Then she remembered. The brake! Her foot had to be on the brake before the car would start. She pressed it to the floor and pushed the start button again, already whimpering with relief.

Nothing happened.

The car door was wrenched open. Duke's growls escalated to a frenzy. She heard his jaws snap together, but they only closed on air.

A woman's voice spoke right in front of her. It was the car, talking to her.

"Cheyenne, this is Ronald."

"Help me!" she screamed. Duke was keeping the man at bay, but how long would that last?

The voice continued under hers without a pause. "We have disabled the vehicle and are coming to get you."

She ran her fingers over the dash, hoping to find a button that would allow her to transmit back. She found several. Which one? She tried mashing them all.

Could they see her? Could they hear her?

"Help me!" she screamed again. "Someone's trying to take me."

Ronald's words, as spoken by the car, continued at the same unhurried pace, uncolored by any emotion other than the exasperated patience of a man being paid by her father. "Please stay with the vehicle."

Duke launched himself out of the car so hard that one of his nails ripped open Cheyenne's jeans. She heard a man's high-pitched scream.

Followed by a gunshot and then a horrible yipping howl.

CHAPTER 18

THE ONLY THING THAT MATTERS

GRIFFIN

Still dressed in the suit Aunt Debby had bought him, Griffin sat on the dirt floor of an abandoned barn surrounded by moldering hay bales. Behind his back, his wrists were handcuffed around a wooden post. Above him, the rotting roof granted him glimpses of a heavy gray sky that matched his mood.

Had his mom's funeral really only been a few hours ago? This whole day had been a nightmare that just got darker by the minute. After the memorial had ended, Griffin had been balancing on his toes on the curb, idly bouncing up and down, when a white box van pulled up next to him. The passenger door swung open.

In the driver's seat was—"Uncle Dwayne?"

"Get in, kid." Dwayne gestured with his big shaved head. "Now."

"But—" Griffin turned to look at Debby. She had her

back to him. Judging by how she was moving her hands, she was still talking.

"I don't have time for this," Dwayne ordered. "Get in."

Only then did Griffin register the fact that Dwayne was pointing a gun at him, almost casually, holding it flat on his thigh. Dwayne and Roy and the other guys had liked to shoot out in the back pasture, the same place Roy had buried the remnants of stolen cars that he couldn't sell. The same place he had buried Griffin's mom after he found her dead.

As he stared at the round empty eye of the gun, Griffin knew that if Dwayne could shoot an empty beer can at twenty yards, he could surely shoot Griffin at one.

Still, he shook his head.

"If you're gonna be that way, I'm going to have to give TJ the signal to take out your aunt."

Griffin followed Dwayne's gaze. Standing a few feet away from Debby was TJ Meadors. Heavier, his hair shorn to his scalp, his stupid rat tail gone. But after all the years TJ had worked for his dad, Griffin would have known him anywhere. In the back pasture, TJ's specialty had been trick shooting: blindfolded, behind his back, or with a gun in each hand like a movie bad guy.

When he saw Griffin looking at him, TJ flashed a grin that lasted just long enough to freeze Griffin's blood. And then he took a step closer to Aunt Debby.

Griffin got in. Even before he was all the way in his

seat, Dwayne was accelerating, the van swaying around a corner hard enough that it closed the door before Griffin could. After some twists and turns, Dwayne stopped in an isolated part of the cemetery that didn't yet hold any graves and ordered Griffin out. When he jumped down to the ground, TJ was just making his way down the hill toward them.

Dwayne kept his gun aimed at Griffin almost casually while TJ patted him down, took his phone, and cuffed his hands behind him. Then they pushed him into the back of the van, which was basically a metal box. With no hands to break his fall, Griffin scraped his forehead pretty bad. He told himself that the wetness he felt on his face was from the blood. Not because of the hopeless position he was in. Not because of the horrifying thing he had seen before the van's doors closed and left him in darkness.

When they finally let him out, he was bruised from rolling around. They each got a hand in an armpit, frog-marched him into the weather-beaten barn, and refastened his handcuffs around a rough wooden post.

Now Dwayne leaned close. His features were bunched together in disgust. "You make me sick! You were going to rat out your own dad!"

Spit landed on Griffin's face, and he had to let it sit there. If Roy sometimes reminded Griffin of a strutting rooster, Dwayne, with his small eyes and bulky body, was more like a pig.

"You don't get it, do you?" Dwayne spoke through gritted teeth. "The only thing that matters in this world is loyalty. Is blood. Your dad is my half brother. Which makes you my half nephew. You should be glad that we share blood, or you would be dead, too."

"So what's he doing here, then?" Griffin jerked his head toward TJ. "He's not blood, but if he's out walking around, you must have got him out."

"He has some skills I can use."

At Dwayne's words, TJ straightened up, an odd grin playing across his face. His stay in the mental hospital did not seem to have improved his mental health.

"Teej, do you think Dwayne really cares about you?" Griffin said, and shook his head. "He's just like Dad, only worse. You must be here so he can use you and then lose you."

Dwayne's slap rocked Griffin's head back into the post so hard that for a second he saw stars.

"Shut up," Dwayne said. "You're the loser here. You were going to get up on that witness stand and do what? Tell the truth? Don't make me laugh. The truth is that you're the one who got your dad into this mess. And the only way you can make up for that is by not testifying. Since you didn't seem to be coming to your senses, I had to step in."

Griffin should have shut up, but he couldn't. "But how's that going to work? Kidnapping me is not going to make them drop kidnapping charges against my dad."

"Who said anything about kidnapping? As far as they know, you got into the van with a friend, said 'later, gator,' and took off on your own."

"They won't believe that." At least Griffin hoped they wouldn't.

TJ laughed. "They already *do* believe it. That ugly aunt of yours was calling your name, and the priest said he saw you getting into a van. She looked really mad."

Debby already worried he was a screwup. Yesterday, she had caught him smoking and yelled at him. Now she must be sure that Uncle Jeff was right, that it had been a big mistake taking him in.

But the other problem with Dwayne's plan was that the case didn't hinge on Griffin. Even without him, Bennett should have no problem prosecuting the case. It was Cheyenne who was the key to his father going to prison. But he wasn't going to remind Dwayne of that fact.

To his horror, his uncle echoed his thoughts. "And don't worry, we've got plans for your little girlfriend, too."

Griffin tried to make his face impassive. He should have realized that this wasn't just about him. It had never been just about him.

They were targeting Cheyenne as well. Cheyenne, the girl he still cared about, even though he had thrown away the second chance she had helped him get.

This was all his fault. Everything was his fault. If he hadn't stolen her stepmom's car, Cheyenne wouldn't have to testify against his dad. If he hadn't startled his dad, his mom would still be alive.

If he hadn't been born, maybe everything and everyone would have been better.

All Griffin knew about Cheyenne and how she was doing now was what he had seen in the media, pictures of her hurrying away from cameras, a baseball cap pulled low, with a woman he didn't think was her stepmom always a half step behind. Sometimes Cheyenne held a cane in her hand; other times it was Phantom's harness.

His stomach churned. He tried to swallow it back down, but bitterness flooded his mouth.

"What are you going to do to her? Kidnap her, too?"

"Don't worry. She's coming to us of her own free will. Or should I say, to you. You're two little lovebirds."

Griffin hated having to ask, hated how it made him look weak, but he didn't have any choice. "I don't understand."

"She's been talking to you on Facebook."

"But I'm not on Facebook." Griffin had joined for a while, back when he was still going to school, but then he had gotten tired of seeing people's happy statuses. Seeing how good their lives were, at least on-screen. It had made him realize just how much his sucked.

Dwayne smirked. "We've been messaging each other on Facebook. Only her photo and her user name belong to her dog. And she thinks I'm you."

Griffin groaned as the implications of what Dwayne was saying sank in.

"She's coming to see you right now." Dwayne pointed a finger at him and then turned it to stab himself in the chest. "And she's going to find me." TJ cleared his throat, and Dwayne amended it to "Find us."

Griffin couldn't let this happen. Not another terrible problem with him at the center. "She'll cause a ruckus if she shows up and finds you instead. If you want to keep her quiet, you should let me help, at least until you can get her out of sight." If they thought he was on their side, he might be able to figure out how they could get away. Or at least how Cheyenne could.

"Good try," Dwayne said, and cuffed his shoulder. Not as hard as the last time he hit him. It might even have been meant to signal affection.

The only reason they hadn't hurt him—so far—was that he was his father's son. Dwayne still had some faint family loyalty to Griffin, at least when it came to spilling blood.

But Cheyenne was a stranger. Her life or death would mean nothing to Dwayne. Instead, she was the one he blamed for this whole mess.

So Griffin thought it likely that once they had her, they would kill her.

The last time Griffin had tried to talk to Cheyenne, six months ago, she had said they couldn't stay in touch. Made it sound like they never could. If he had known that she might change her mind, would that have changed things for him? Would he have been more rooted, less rudderless?

A few hours after it got dark, Dwayne and TJ left. Before they did, Dwayne slapped duct tape across Griffin's mouth to keep him quiet.

Griffin had seen a mouse caught in a glue trap once. Squirming, trying to get its feet free. Trying so hard that its heart finally gave out and it slumped over.

That's how Griffin felt now. In the dark, he twisted his hands. He was careful not to press the cuffs against anything. He had already discovered the hard way that if you did that, the cuff would ratchet tighter. But there was still some room in the right one. And to get out of here, all he needed to do was get out of one. If he could just fold his thumb in tight enough. His wrists were wet with sweat. Or blood. If he could use the wetness to lubricate the cuffs, then maybe he could scrape them off.

Maybe.

He just knew he couldn't give up.

CHAPTER 19

ANOTHER VICTIM

CHEYENNE

The car door was wrenched open, and strong hands dragged Cheyenne out. She screamed, even though she knew there was no one to hear. No one but Duke, and he was dead.

As soon as she got her feet under her, she put her right hand on top of her attacker's, just as Jaydra had taught her. Because she could feel his thumb, she knew how he was standing in relation to her. She began to twist the wrist he was holding so that she could grip his forearm with the same arm he had just grabbed, all the while keeping his hand pressed against her wrist. Done correctly, it would break his wrist.

But, Cheyenne realized a second too late, there was another man behind her.

The second man wrenched her right arm back, his breath hot on her neck as he pushed it up between her shoulder blades. Cold metal ratcheted around her wrist. A handcuff. As long as he had only one of her wrists, she might still be able to escape. She tried to twist free. But the man just grabbed her other wrist and forced it behind her. The second cuff snapped closed.

Lacing her fingers together to make her hands as bony as possible, Cheyenne tried to strike him in the crotch. Her only reward was a coarse laugh in her ear.

"You nearly broke my wrist!" the man in front of her said. Amazement colored his high-pitched voice.

Cheyenne recognized it immediately from her nightmares. TJ Meadors. Found too crazy to participate in his own trial. Although apparently not too crazy to figure out how to escape the mental hospital.

"You killed Duke!"

"That wasn't me. It was Dwayne!"

So the man behind her wasn't Roy, even if he sounded a lot like him.

"Stop yakking and help me carry her," Dwayne commanded.

When TJ's hands fumbled at her ankles, Cheyenne managed to kick him under the chin, making him grunt and stagger back. She tried to wrench free from Dwayne, but he just grabbed her under the arms. And this time when TJ bent down to seize her ankles, he succeeded.

They lifted her into the air and began to carry her. Cheyenne twisted and bucked, hoping to get at least one foot free. With one foot, she could kick again. Given one foot, she might gain two. And then she could run. Her collapsible cane was still in her pocket, although there was probably no way to use it with her hands cuffed behind her.

But when they finally let her go, it was to throw her into a vehicle. The metal floor made a hollow sound when she landed painfully on her left shoulder. A door banged closed, trapping her inside.

"Go get her purse out of the car and bring it back here," Dwayne said on the other side of the door. "But first turn off her phone."

"Sure," TJ said. "I want to check out that car." He sounded eager.

"There's no time for that. They're coming for her, and we need to get out of here before they show up. Just get her purse, turn off her phone, and that's all."

She willed TJ to argue, but instead he was silent. A few seconds later, through the walls of her new prison, she heard the front doors of the vehicle open and close. The engine started up, and then they began to move.

Cheyenne lay on her side, panting openmouthed. Her heart was a broken-winged bird trapped in the cage of her ribs.

She took stock. She had been kidnapped. Handcuffed. She was in the back of some kind of delivery van. At least it wasn't the trunk of a car, she told herself. The space was bigger than that. She could move around, maybe figure out a way to surprise the two men when they opened the door again. Through the front wall, she could hear them talking to each other, but the sounds were muffled.

What she couldn't let herself think about was how she had ended up here. About how Griffin had betrayed her.

All those things he had messaged her had been lies. About how he missed her and thought she was beautiful and couldn't wait to see her again. Even back in the woods, it must all have been a lie. He must have encouraged her to keep going knowing his dad would catch her. Griffin hadn't expected her to turn the tables on Roy.

He had spun a pretty web of lies, and she had thrown herself into it. Just as her dad and Danielle had warned her, Griffin would always be his father's son. Her guilt at having tried to kill him must have colored how she remembered things in the woods. The Griffin she remembered, the Griffin she had built up in her head—that Griffin did not exist.

The van took a sharp turn, and Cheyenne rolled into something.

Not something. *Someone.*

She let out a screech and pushed herself away.

"Hello? Who are you?"

No answer. But it had to be another victim. Maybe too traumatized to speak.

"Talk to me. Maybe the two of us can figure out a way to get out of here. I can't see you because I'm blind."

She held her breath, waiting for a word or a whisper, but none came. With a sickening twist of the gut, she recalled what she had barely registered when she first felt it. Whatever—whoever—it was had been covered by a stiff and crackly layer. Plastic of some kind.

Cheyenne managed to sit up. Even though her hands were cuffed behind her, she needed them to tell her if what she was afraid of was true. She found she could scoot backward if she pointed her hands straight toward her bottom, transferred her weight to her palms and heels, and then inched herself back. Each time she repositioned her hands, she first patted the air behind her. Finally her fingers touched whatever it was she had rolled against.

With one finger, she poked it again. It gave a little at her touch. Definitely flesh, wrapped up in what felt like a plastic tarp. Trembling, she ran her palm over the part she was closest to. Something round, maybe four inches across. It did not move in response to her handling. And she registered what she hadn't before—that the flesh under the tarp was cool.

So whatever she was touching was dead. Could it be an animal? A dead animal? Cheyenne thought of the gunshot and the terrible sound Duke had made. Could they have wrapped up his body and thrown it inside right before they came for her?

But wouldn't he still be warm? Besides, Cheyenne didn't think it was an animal. It was too big. Too big to be anything but a person. Was it another girl? A dead girl? As she would be soon?

Then she had another thought, even worse. Did the body belong to Griffin? Had they tricked him into helping them and then killed him when they didn't need him anymore?

Cheyenne had to know. She couldn't bear to know. But she had to.

Or—the thought filled her with a surge of hope— maybe she was imagining it, thinking that something so large had to be human. Maybe it was a deer, shot out of season. That thing she had thought was an arm might have been a deer's slender leg. Maybe.

The more rational part of her brain reminded her that it was more likely Griffin. At the thought, it was as if she could see the Griffin she had built in her mind, the Griffin with dark hair and dark eyes and the scar around his neck, lying pale and still beneath a blue plastic tarp.

Her thoughts ran in circles until finally they stopped altogether. She forced herself to grab a fold of tarp and tug. Scoot forward and tug, scoot forward and tug, until she felt the tarp slide halfway off. Then she scooted back to the body.

Disturbing the tarp had released the metallic smell of blood. It filled her nostrils, stronger even than the smell of the diesel exhaust.

Cheyenne lifted her hands as high as she could and then slowly brought her palms down.

It was an arm. Definitely an arm, not some animal's leg. She swiped her fingers sideways to be sure and touched cool, curled fingers. A whimper was ripped from her throat.

She crabbed farther up. She needed to feel the face. No matter how much she feared it.

But when she reached out, she touched the chest. It was definitely a man, the chest muscled and flat. Blood sticky beneath her fingers. Her index finger slipped into a small hole. With a cry she pulled it out. Whoever it was, he had been shot to death.

She scooted higher, found the dead man's face. Her fingers traced a strong nose. Griffin's nose had been strong. As tears burned her eyes, she made herself amend the thought. Yes, Griffin had a strong nose. So did a lot of men. That didn't mean this was Griffin.

And underneath the nose, her fingers found a mustache. The last time she had seen Griffin he had been clean shaven. And he was only seventeen. This mustache was so bristly it felt like it had been growing for years. Cheyenne traced its shape with her fingers. It bracketed the mouth and went all the way down to the chin in a narrow line on either side. Not a typical shape for a mustache.

But something about it was familiar. Familiar from before, from when she had still been able to see. Someone in her life had had a mustache like that.

And then it came to her. Danielle talking about Octavio. Thinking he must be sick. Why he wasn't answering his phone.

Now Cheyenne knew the answer. It was Octavio who was dead in this van, not another girl, not Griffin. Which meant she had to accept the truth—that Griffin had lied to her, lured her to what most likely would be her death.

When the van went around a sharp turn, she lost her balance and tipped over next to Octavio's body. She curled up in a fetal position and let the tears come.

CHAPTER 20

RUN AWAY SCREAMING

CHEYENNE

Cheyenne heard Jaydra's voice in her head. *A small amount of adrenaline can help you. Too much prepares you to die.*

When she had set out to save Griffin, Cheyenne's adrenaline must have been in what Jaydra said was the yellow zone, which left you ready to fight, but still able to think. Once the men showed up, she had entered the red zone, her body no longer analyzing, just reacting. Now she lay curled on the metal floor of the van, a fine tremble washing over her. Without urgency, Cheyenne thought she must be moving into the gray zone, where she would be unable to think, and barely able to act.

She vaguely knew that she needed to get things under control before she went into the black zone, where she would lose even gross motor skills. Jaydra said the black zone was meant to be protective, your body's last-ditch effort to keep you from being noticed, or at least from doing something stupid. She would be frozen, in shock. Unable to do anything while the men could do whatever they wanted to her.

That thought finally reached Cheyenne. The idea of TJ touching her, murmuring into her ear the way he had six months ago, shot through her like an electric shock. No! She couldn't let that happen.

The antidote to adrenaline is oxygen, Jaydra whispered in her head. *Remember your four-count breathing.* Four counts in, hold four counts, four counts out, hold four counts. It would stop her adrenaline from spiking to the point where it rendered her useless.

Cheyenne forced herself to breathe from her belly until she stopped shaking, stopped hearing her heartbeat slamming in her ears. She twisted her hand until she could check her Braille watch. It was a few minutes after two in the morning. She had been in the back of the van for about twenty minutes.

With a groan, she pushed herself to a sitting position. She needed to get out of these handcuffs before the men opened the door to the van. Jaydra had warned her about what she called the increasing quality of incarceration. *First you're in handcuffs in the trunk of a car. Then you'll be in a locked room chained by your ankle to a bed. Every time you change locations, it will be harder to escape. So the sooner you do, the better.*

Jaydra said the first step was to take stock of what you had on hand that you could use to help yourself. But

Cheyenne didn't have anything. Her purse was up front with the men. The fob, which was heavy enough it might have had some utility, was back in the car. In the pockets of her raincoat were just her folded cane, some plastic bags for dog poop, and a handful of kibble.

Kibble made her think of Duke, of how he had died trying to protect her. She forced herself to blink away the tears. She didn't have time for them now.

Jaydra always carried a handcuff key tucked behind the label on her pants, held in place with Velcro. When she had told Cheyenne that, she had thought it was the most ridiculous, paranoid thing she had ever heard. She had drawn the line at that, so Jaydra had encouraged her to always clip her hair back with a bobby pin or metal hair clip that could be broken and repurposed. Unfortunately, Cheyenne hadn't listened to that advice, either.

Jaydra had taught Cheyenne how to get out of duct tape and zip ties and ropes, but they had spent the most time on handcuffs. If you knew what you were doing, you could open them using almost any small, thin piece of metal: bobby pins, safety pins, binder clips, paper clips, even a dipstick. One way was to use the metal as a shim. You slid it between the cuff and the bumpy part—the rachet. As you pressed both the cuff and the shim in, the piece of metal would block the teeth of the ratchet so that you could swing the cuff open. Or you could bend the piece of metal in a specific way and use it like a handcuff key. *Handcuffs are simply a control device,* Jaydra had said. *They're not meant to keep you permanently locked up. The design hasn't changed much for a century, and they all work the same way.*

It had been fun to figure out how to do it, but once Cheyenne had, her interest had diminished. It all seemed like crazy overkill.

At least until now.

Then she thought of her coat. It closed with a zipper. And the zipper pull was small, flat, and made of metal. Maybe she could use it to shim open the cuffs! Her heart thrilled until she twisted enough to touch it. It was far too wide. She checked the one on her pants. It was smaller, but still too wide to fit between the notched edge of the rachet and the handcuff.

Her only hope was that sometime in the van's years of use, some small piece of metal had landed on the floor and been left there. Starting in one corner, she began to search, sweeping with her fingers. With each pass, she overlapped the area she'd just swept. But all too soon, she had to acknowledge that there was nothing she could use, either to get out of her cuffs or as a weapon. No thin pieces of metal. No jumper cables. Not even a handy bag of wrenches.

The van was empty, except for her and Octavio.

That left Octavio.

If touching Octavio's face and the bullet hole in his

chest had been bad, searching through his pockets was going to be worse. And tricky, since Cheyenne had to work behind her back with her hands cuffed together. She muttered, "Sorry," as she started to worm her fingers into the pants pocket nearest her.

She almost immediately forgot her unease when her fingers touched something metal. Slowly, she tugged it free, traced its shape as it made a faint musical noise. A key ring, but it held only keys, and its metal ring was too thick and rigid to use on her handcuffs. If she could ever get her hands free, she could slip the keys between the fingers of her fist to use like claws. But that was a pretty big if. Still, Cheyenne contorted herself until she could push it into her own righthand pocket.

To get to Octavio's far pocket, she had to stretch out on his torso.

And when she did, he let out a gurgle.

With a shriek, Cheyenne scrambled away. Octavio couldn't still be alive.

Could he?

After a long moment, she forced herself to go back.

She held her hand over his mouth and nose for a count of ten. *One Mississippi, two Mississippi.* . . . But no breath stirred against her palm. When she gently touched his face again, it felt like cool wax. She must have released some air still trapped in his lungs.

She returned to her search, but Octavio's left pocket was empty. And his back pockets held only his wallet.

A few minutes later, the van began to slow and she readied herself. She needed to get away before the situation got even worse. Before she ended up like Octavio. As soon as they opened up the back, she would try to run away screaming. But when the van door opened and she tried to scramble out, a fist punched her in the temple.

A flash of white light zigzagged through her head.

And then all the lights went out.

CHAPTER 21

MAKE A KILLING

CHEYENNE

A minute or an hour later, Cheyenne woke up. Or, she realized as she struggled to raise her lolling head, that wasn't exactly it. She was coming to. She was sitting with her legs straight out in front of her, her back propped against something narrow and rough. A spot on the side of her head throbbed in time with her heart. It felt wet. She started to lift her hand to touch it, but was stopped short. Her hands were still cuffed behind her, only this time they were around a post.

It all came back to her in a rush. Hearing TJ and a man who sounded like Roy, and then the horrible noise Duke made when he was shot. Touching Octavio's face in the van. Struggling with the men when the van finally stopped. Pain blooming as a fist struck her. And then nothing.

They had brought her here. Wherever here was. Someplace they didn't think anyone would look for her. Her skin crawled. Were they watching her right now? She didn't hear anything.

Cheyenne closed her eyes, let her head drop back to her chest, and forced her body to go slack. Maybe she could buy herself some time so she could figure out just how bad things were.

Where was she? Before she had closed her eyes, her left eye, with its little slice of vision, had revealed nothing but blackness.

Had more than time vanished with that blow to the head? Three years ago, being thrown against a pole by a careening car had destroyed most of her sight. Had she just lost what little remained? Her stomach bottomed out. It was all she could do to remain limp.

She hovered on the edge of panic, of screaming and thrashing, even though it would do no good. Again, she forced herself to breathe, to slowly count to four over and over. As she quietly, rhythmically inhaled and exhaled, Cheyenne took inventory. The post she was handcuffed to was made of rough wood. The ground under her felt like hard-packed dirt. The air smelled of cigarette smoke, mildew, hay, and—she inhaled even more deeply— manure. Far overhead, rain pattered against the roof.

Some kind of barn or stable? Maybe abandoned, given the mildew and that the sweet smell of dung was very faint, more a memory than a scent. Cheyenne strained her ears, but didn't hear any sounds, not even of traffic.

Ronald and her dad must have found the car by now. But would they realize that Cheyenne wasn't there because she had been taken? Since TJ had retrieved her purse, they might think she had left the car willingly, maybe been picked up by a Good Samaritan. They might not know to call the cops.

Then she remembered Duke. When they found him dead of a gunshot wound, it would be a pretty good clue that something was very wrong.

Her eyes and nose began to fill with tears at thoughts of Duke and Octavio. Of her dad and Danielle. If only she had hugged them hard before she left tonight. As she mourned what she hadn't done and what she would never be, she felt the faintest of tickles on her neck. Then it moved a millimeter higher.

Something was *crawling* on her.

Forgetting all about pretending to still be knocked out, Cheyenne shrugged her shoulder toward her cheek, frantically trying to wipe off whatever it was

"Morning, honey bunny." The voice she heard was the man TJ had called Dwayne. Was it really morning? She twisted her hands so she could touch her Braille watch. It was just before three A.M.

No sense in pretending to still be unconscious. "Who are you? You sound like Roy, but you're not."

"Aren't you smart?" It was clear this wasn't a compliment. "You would have had them eating out of your hand in court." He made his voice singsong like a carnival barker's. "She might be blind, folks, but she's pretty and has supersenses. Hears a voice and knows who it's related to." She heard the flick of a lighter, a suck of breath as he lit a cigarette. "I'm Dwayne. Roy's my half brother."

"Why did you kill Octavio?"

"He was going to work for us. But then he got cold feet. And then cold everything else." Dwayne exhaled showily, and she imagined twin streams of smoke coming out of his nose.

Everyone was dying because of her. "Where's Griffin?" Had he betrayed her, or was he among the dead?

"Do you really think he was going to let his dad go to prison? What was it you told him again? 'Just tell me where you are and promise you'll wait for me.' You should have seen him laughing."

To her right, something stirred, but Cheyenne paid no attention. Dwayne's words had stolen all the breath from her lungs.

"This was all Griffin's idea," he continued. "He's mad at you for how you were going to put away his dad. Of course, that's not going to happen now."

Griffin must have shared her messages. About how she missed him, thought about him, longed for him. Had Dwayne been sitting next to him, laughing as they composed his replies together? Her sense of betrayal was so great that it was all Cheyenne could do not to throw up.

She had been such a fool. She had thrown herself into their arms. And now she was trussed up like an animal ready to be slaughtered.

"You're probably the first person in history who ever kidnapped herself," Dwayne said. "And in such a nice car. Too bad we couldn't keep it. TJ could barely tear himself away."

"I've seen them self-driving cars on TV," TJ said, "but I never thought I would get to look at one up close." His voice was filled with longing. The last time Cheyenne had heard TJ sound like that, he had been stroking her cheek.

Cheyenne tried to keep her fear from showing on her face. For the last six months, TJ had occupied a lot of her nightmares. His fingertip tracing the line of her jaw as he whispered in her ear the things he wanted to do to her. She hoped that he had left lots of fingerprints on the car. And that the police would think to look for them.

"Go outside and keep watch," Dwayne told TJ.

As Dwayne had been talking, Cheyenne had been exploring. She had turned her wrists so that her hands were flat against the floor behind her. Slowly, slowly, she was fanning her fingers across the rough surface. The only thing she found was loose straw. All she needed was a tiny piece of metal, and it seemed more likely that she would find one here than in the van. Didn't hay come trussed in baling wire?

"You'll tell me when you're done?" TJ sounded eager.

Done with what?

"No worries. Later, gator."

She had been an idiot, she thought as her fingers pressed and probed behind her back. She remembered an old *New Yorker* cartoon her dad had shown her before she went blind. It pictured a dog sitting in a chair in front of a computer, saying to another dog sitting on the floor, "On the Internet, nobody knows you're a dog."

Cheyenne would have been a lot better off if she had been messaging a dog. Dogs didn't pretend one thing and do another. Dogs didn't betray you.

"Why'd you have to shoot Duke?"

"What—you mean besides him biting me?" She heard the shrug in Dwayne's voice. "He got exactly what he deserved. He was my brother's dog and then he took off with you."

Cheyenne took a deep shuddering breath, trying to suppress her tears. As she did, she felt whatever had been on her neck start to move again, crossing the line of her jaw. Raising her shoulder, she tried to wipe it off her cheek.

"Okay, here's the deal. We're going to make a little film for your dad. And you're going to be the star. Isn't that every girl's dream? To be a movie star?"

Cheyenne's attention was divided, half on Dwayne,

half on the delicate legs walking up her cheek. She twisted her lips and blew as hard as she could in the bug's direction, but the steady sense of movement didn't falter.

"What's the matter?" Dwayne came closer. Her left eye picked up a sliver of bobbing white light. Her relief at not having lost her tiny slice of vision was cut short when his bitter breath washed over her face. A hand cupped her chin. She tried to jerk away, but he squeezed the sides of her jaw to hold her still, then forcefully tilted her head. "Awesome, possum. Looks like you've already made a little friend." His hand smelled of cigarettes. She pressed her lips together and tried to breathe shallowly.

When his other hand touched her face, she expected him to brush off the bug. Instead, he squished it with his thumb.

Bile flooded her mouth as he pressed so hard against her cheek that Cheyenne was sure there would be a bruise there tomorrow. If there was a tomorrow.

He finally let her go. She tried to rub the crushed bug off on her shoulder, but couldn't reach the spot.

"Leave it. You'll look more pathetic. And if your daddy paid a million last time, just think how much more he'll be willing to give now, when he'll be able to see you. He'll take one look at you, handcuffed, with blood on your temple and a smashed spider on your cheek, and he'll be more than willing to pay three million. We're going to make a killing. Except we'll do it a little smarter than my brother did. Small unmarked bills take time to get your hands on, and they take up a lot of space. So last decade. Your dad's going to put money in an untraceable Bitcoin account. Once we get it, we're gonna let you go. Okeydokey, artichokey?"

Dwayne seemed to be waiting for an answer, so Cheyenne nodded. That hadn't been true when Roy asked for ransom. And she was sure it wasn't true now. Once they got the money, she would have served her purpose.

Alive, she could testify. Dead, she would be silent forever.

CHAPTER 22

LET'S SEE JUST HOW LOUD YOU CAN SCREAM

GRIFFIN

With duct tape over his mouth, Griffin had been forced to listen in silence as Dwayne told Cheyenne lies about his supposed betrayal. As he spoke, Dwayne's eyes darted back and forth between them, a smile playing around his lips.

Tears of frustration sprang into Griffin's eyes. He blinked them away. If his nose started to run, he would smother.

Even though she must feel so alone and frightened, it didn't show in Cheyenne's face, which was half obscured by her mass of dark curls. The only light came from a large flashlight lying on top of a hay bale and pointing directly at her. She was more petite than Griffin remembered. Next to Dwayne, she looked like a child.

This was all his fault. If Griffin hadn't reached out to her six months ago, she wouldn't have believed Dwayne when he had pretended to be Griffin on Facebook. Now he would do anything to save her. But he couldn't even save himself. The panic about what would happen to both of them squirmed inside him.

"First, I need you to memorize the account number," Dwayne told Cheyenne. He rattled off a string of about a dozen letters and numbers, then started again with the first four. "Say those back to me."

After she did, he made her repeat them over and over. Then he added two more. They went back and forth. Each time she got a sequence of numbers right, he added a couple more. When Cheyenne messed up, he took it back a step or two.

Griffin wondered if she was stalling for time. Would it help if she did? She kept fidgeting, moving her legs and shrugging her shoulders. Griffin knew firsthand just how uncomfortable their positions were, but as he watched her, he wondered if something else was going on. From this angle, it seemed like she was running her fingers over the ground behind her. What was she looking for? There was nothing in this abandoned barn but musty hay.

Finally she was able to recite the whole string of numbers and letters from memory.

Dwayne took out his phone. "Okay, I'm going to film you now. Make this look good. You're scared, and the only one who can save you is your daddy—and his money. Ready, Freddy? Three, two, one . . . Action!"

She sucked in a breath, her eyes not quite pointed in

Dwayne's direction. "Daddy, I'm okay. I love you and Danielle so much. And I'm sorry about everything. Tell Ronald I'm sorry I took—"

His lip curling, Dwayne stabbed his finger at his phone to turn off the camera. His voice overrode hers. "Stop, stop. You don't sound scared at all. Your dad's going to watch this and think you're just fine, that you're just kicking back."

Cheyenne cringed. "I'll try to do better."

"I don't need you to try," Dwayne said. "I need you to DO. I need you to sound scared out of your mind." When she nodded, he started again. "Three, two, one . . . Action!"

When Cheyenne spoke, her voice was pitched higher. To Griffin, it sounded like she was holding back tears. "Daddy, I'm really scared. Please give them the money. Please! As soon as you do, they'll let me go."

"No! No!" Dwayne's voice cut through hers. "That's nowhere near good enough. It doesn't sound real at all. We want your dad falling all over himself to transfer the money to us."

She shifted again, moving an inch or two around the pole. From where he sat, Griffin could see her hands, but Dwayne couldn't. Her fingers kept creeping over the hard-packed earth. What was she looking for?

Cheyenne raised her chin. "I'm doing the best I can."

Dwayne shook his head. "Oh, I think you could do a

lot better than that. You might not care about a spider, but I'm sure you do know how much a burn hurts. Let's see just how loud you can scream. And trust me, no one but us will be able to hear you."

Dwayne took his lighter from his pocket. Griffin tried to shout, but nothing came out but a faint, strangled sound. For a moment, Cheyenne's face swiveled in Griffin's direction, but when Dwayne flicked on his lighter, she quickly turned back.

"No, please, don't!"

Dwayne looked from the wavering yellow flame to her. "You should have thought of that before you sicced Duke on me or slammed my hand in the door."

With his other hand, he took out a fresh cigarette and lit it. Then he flipped his lighter closed and slipped it back in his pocket.

Griffin was starting to relax, to tell himself Dwayne's threat had just been meant to scare her, when Dwayne pinched the cigarette between his fingers, leaned down, and held it only an inch or two from Cheyenne's face. She must have felt the round dot of heat, because she froze. He held it over her cheek, then her forehead, as if he was trying to decide the best spot. He brought it closer. She twisted her head, but the post stopped her from going very far. The cigarette edged closer and closer to her temple, until Griffin was sure her skin must be starting to crisp.

"No, no!" Cheyenne said. "Don't! I'll do better, I promise!"

Dwayne paused. "A few marks here and there will only make your dad more of an eager beaver. Years ago, there was this rich kid. A Getty. The kidnappers chopped off an ear and sent it to his folks. You can bet that made them get off their fat butts and hurry up the ransom." Without warning, he crouched and pressed the burning cigarette onto her left hand.

Cheyenne screamed, and so did Griffin, the sound stoppered behind the duct tape. This was all his fault. Dwayne must have chosen this method to torture her knowing that watching her be burned would be almost as hard on Griffin.

TJ yanked open the barn door and ran inside yelling. "Stop it! Stop it!" He leaned down and knocked the cigarette out of Dwayne's hand.

Dwayne straightened up. He was a head and a half taller than TJ, but TJ wasn't backing down. The smell of burning flesh—it stank like burning hair—hung in the air. It made bile rise in Griffin's throat as a million terrible memories came flooding back.

Cheyenne had stopped screaming. She panted open-mouthed, her face red and wet with tears.

"You said you wouldn't hurt her!" TJ protested.

"Keep your pants on. She's not really hurt. It was all

just for dramatic effect." Dwayne shrugged. "I needed to get her crying so her daddy will send the money faster."

"He burned my hand!" Cheyenne's voice was filled with pain and panic.

TJ knelt next to her, his face creased with concern. Griffin froze. Both TJ and Dwayne scared him, but in different ways. Dwayne at least made a rough kind of sense, but TJ had always lived in his own world. To Griffin, it seemed equally likely that right now TJ would kiss Cheyenne or kill her. Maybe both.

"Are you all right?" TJ pushed a strand of hair from Cheyenne's face. She shuddered at his touch.

"Hey, that's perfect!" Dwayne was grinning. "She's shaking like a leaf, obviously scared and crying. And then we show a man's hand reaching out and caressing her face all lovey-dovey. They'll be buying those Bitcoins before they're even done watching the video. Let's try that again. TJ, move back a little, so that when you reach in to touch her, they won't see your face. Ready, Cheyenne?" He didn't wait for her to answer. "Three, two, one, and action!"

Cheyenne said in a trembling voice, "Please, Daddy, please." As TJ's hand stroked her cheek, her face contorted with disgust and fear. "Please help me. They want three million dollars, and it has to be in Bitcoins. If you don't give it to them, they're going to kill me. You have to send it to this account." She rattled off the number without making a single mistake. "Please send it right away. I love you."

"Okay, cut!"

TJ didn't move away. Instead he picked up Cheyenne's limp hand and leaned down to gently kiss the burn.

Griffin heard Cheyenne gag. TJ made a sound of disgust and scooted back. Turning her head to the other side, Cheyenne spit. When she lifted her head, she said to Dwayne, "I thought you were supposed to be doing this to help your brother. But they're going to guess he's behind this. Who else would have a reason for wanting to kidnap me?"

Dwayne shrugged. "Just wait until they get an anonymous tip about your secret Facebook account. They'll see all your messages back and forth with Griffin, and they'll know that you two ran off together. Then the trial will be postponed—forever." He laughed without mirth. "And to make sure they get the point, I just need you to make one more recording."

Cheyenne lifted her chin. "I don't think I can sound any more scared than I just did."

"Don't worry. That last one was just perfect. This one needs a different tone, but I swear it will be easy-peasy. We just need to get you cleaned up." He directed his next words to TJ. "Use the tail of your shirt to wipe her face clean."

Cheyenne seemed frozen as TJ gingerly swabbed her face. Then he combed his fingers through her hair, shaking his hand free every time he caught a snag.

"Okay, that looks pretty good," Dwayne said. "Now put a smile on your face, Cheyenne. And when I say 'action,' I need you to say something like, 'Sorry I had to fool you guys, Daddy, but I'm tired of being treated like a helpless little girl. Griffin and I need money so we can be on our own.'"

Griffin saw how it would go. Cheyenne's dad and stepmom would watch the second video when Dwayne sent it after getting the money. They would read her Facebook conversations with what everyone would think was him. And they would be convinced that she was on the lam with Griffin, happily spending Nick's millions.

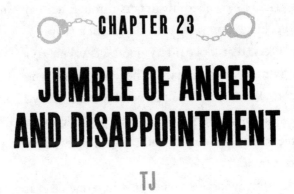

CHAPTER 23

JUMBLE OF ANGER AND DISAPPOINTMENT

TJ

Three hours before TJ and Dwayne had taken Cheyenne, they had stopped to fill up the stolen van's gas tank. TJ went into the men's bathroom. Ignoring the stench, he brushed his teeth with his index finger, swished water around his mouth, and spit it out.

Just knowing he was going to see Cheyenne again made him feel like something was reverberating inside him. Like listening to music so loud you could feel it in your rib cage.

He had imagined being with her so many times, in so many different ways. Slow dancing together. Picnicking on a bluff overlooking the ocean. Laughing in bed, the white sheet pulled over them like a tent.

Now Cheyenne sat slumped on the dirt floor, her still-tangled hair hanging over her face. The flashlight propped on a disintegrating hay bale was focused on her. She looked nothing like the girl TJ had thought about for so many months.

Were the things he had dreamed about only dreams? Back when he was taking the rainbow pills in the hospital, they had made sense. But what if they had really been lies? Or, what if it wasn't the dreams that were a lie, but . . . her?

No, TJ told himself, it was only what Dwayne had done to her. How he had treated her. How he had hurt her. Dwayne had acted like it was no big deal, just a little encouragement to get her to seem scared. But Cheyenne definitely hadn't been pretending. Plus TJ knew from personal experience how much cigarette burns hurt. And he'd seen the hungry look in Dwayne's eyes when he burned her. If he hadn't knocked the cigarette away, would Dwayne have seared her skin with even more?

"Come look at this." With his chin, Dwayne motioned TJ over to join him. He was standing in front of the box van's passenger door, open for the illumination of the dome light. The van was parked just inside the sliding barn door. They had found this place in the daylight, not thinking about how dark it would be at night, with no power.

"I'll bet when her dad sees this video, he'll have the Bitcoins in our account in under an hour."

Dwayne pressed the play button on his phone as TJ leaned in closer. On the screen, Cheyenne looked even more pathetic, eyes brimming with tears. His own hand entered the screen. TJ flushed. His knuckles were always black in the creases with engine oil, no matter how much he scrubbed them. Then his gaze shifted to Cheyenne's recorded face. He had only been trying to comfort her, but now he saw that when he had touched her, she had pulled back, her expression mingling disgust and horror.

He reminded himself that she couldn't see anything. She must have thought he was Dwayne.

The clip ended. "Isn't that perfect?" Dwayne slid the phone into his pocket. "I'm going into town to send this. Just in case they manage to trace it back, I want it to lead someplace anonymous with an open Wi-Fi connection, like a hotel."

TJ didn't really follow what Dwayne was talking about, but he knew what was expected of him. What was always expected of him. All he needed to do was nod and agree.

"Okay."

"I should be back in about an hour, maybe a little more."

From the corner behind them, Cheyenne spoke. "Wait, what? Are you going to leave me alone with TJ? Please, please, don't do that."

In the opposite corner, Griffin gagged. Handcuffed to another post, he was also violently shaking his head, his eyes wide. TJ didn't pay him any attention, and neither did Dwayne, but they both turned to look at Cheyenne. She cocked her head and turned it in Griffin's direction.

"No worries," Dwayne said. "I'm sure he'll leave you alone. And if he doesn't? Well, he knows not to leave any marks—at least not any that will show on camera. Don't you, TJ?"

"Are you going to leave me the handcuff key?" TJ asked hopefully.

Dwayne patted his shirt pocket. "I'm afraid that stays with me, buddy."

TJ helped him get the barn door open and then slid it back in place after he drove away. Then he walked slowly over to Cheyenne.

Her red T-shirt set off her dark hair. It was the exact same color as Superman's cape. When TJ was eight, his favorite cartoon show in the whole world had been *Super Friends*. The commercial breaks urged you to buy all the action figures: Batman, Wonder Woman, Aquaman. . . . But TJ only had eyes for Superman. Superman could fly! He wouldn't stop pestering his mom until finally she broke down and got it for him for Christmas.

He remembered ripping the green wrapping paper off the box, seeing Superman in his red cape with the large S on his chest.

But the thing was, Superman didn't actually fly. TJ tried helpfully flinging him into the air, but every single time, he came down like a rock, his cape not even fluttering a little bit.

"What did you think was going to happen, dummy?" his mom said, and then sucked hard on her cigarette.

He didn't bother answering, but the next time she left him alone while she went out, he took one of the kitchen knives to Superman. When she came home, she found Superman's torso lying on its back on the coffee table. His severed head sat on top of the S, and his arms and legs were stacked neatly to one side.

That was when his mom started locking TJ in his room. Even when she was home.

As he walked over to Cheyenne, her eyes followed him, but it had to be her ears that told her where he was. He dropped to his knees, and she flinched.

"Why don't you like me?" TJ said. It broke his heart a little that he had to ask her that.

Instead of answering, she said, "Dwayne's going to kill me. As soon as he has the money, he will kill me." Sweat was beaded along her hairline.

"No he won't. That's just pretend, to make your dad pay."

"Think about it. Why did you guys take me?"

"So I could be with you." When TJ saw Cheyenne's shoulders hunch in a shiver, he added, "Do you want my puffer coat?" Summer hadn't really come in yet. Maybe when it did, he would finally get warm. In his mind's eye, he saw the two of them lying on a beach, the yellow sun beating down.

She shook her head. "No, I don't want your coat. I want you to think. Why else did you guys take me?"

"To get the money from your dad. And so you won't testify against Roy."

"Right. And once he gets the money, Dwayne will want to make absolutely sure that I'm never able to testify. And the only way he can do that is to kill me." She blinked and fresh tears ran down her cheeks.

He wiped them away with his index finger. Her skin, which he had thought would be like velvet, was slick with tears and even some snot. A girl like Cheyenne shouldn't even make snot.

Still, he hurried to reassure her. "That's not going to happen. You and me, we'll just go someplace really far away. An island or something. And each one of us will have one-third of the money. A million dollars! Do you know what we could do with so much money?" TJ was a little hazy on the details himself, but the way Dwayne talked about the money, his voice soft with longing, he knew it was good.

Cheyenne swore. "Do you really believe that? He'll probably kill both of us. Make it look like a murder-suicide. And then he'll have all the money to himself."

"That's not going to happen!" TJ wished she would just be quiet. The more she talked, the harder it was to remember why he had wanted her. Leaning closer, he sniffed, but she didn't smell the sweet way he remembered. The way she smelled reminded him of the mental hospital. Of vomit and of rank, anxious sweat.

"You just need to relax, Cheyenne. I'll take care of everything. I'll take care of you." Bracing one hand on the pole next to her head, he closed his eyes, conjuring up the Cheyenne of his memory, and then leaned in to kiss her. At the last second, she turned her head away. His lips landed on her jaw.

He had thought that because Cheyenne couldn't see him, she would be different from other girls. The ones who always looked more than a little disgusted by him.

She turned her head even farther, and before he knew what was happening, her teeth had closed on his wrist.

He yelped and tried to shake her off. Finally he had to slap her head to get her to loosen her teeth. He stared at his wrist in disbelief. Her teeth had left holes. In him! Blood shone on her lips. His blood.

It was all going wrong. All those nights, he had imagined finally being with Cheyenne again. But in his dreams, she hadn't been like this girl, dirty, scratched, snotty, foulmouthed. Violent.

"You bit me!" He was mesmerized by the red welling up. He didn't like blood, but when it was his own, that made him crazy. He raised his hands, ready to slip them around her throat. Ready to squeeze and squeeze.

From the far corner came a noise. It sounded like Griffin was choking. TJ looked over. Griffin's back was arched, and his heels drummed against the floor. Was he choking to death?

Griffin had always treated him okay. TJ finally got up, walked away from Cheyenne, and pulled the tape from Griffin's mouth.

But instead of thanking TJ, Griffin said between heaving breaths, "If you hurt her, Dwayne will kill you. You've got to keep her alive until you get the money. What if they won't send the money until they have a video of her saying what day it is or something?"

"But she bit me!"

"Yeah, and if you hurt her," Griffin insisted, "Dwayne will kill you."

"Shut up!" TJ's thoughts were a jumble of anger and disappointment. "Just shut up! Let me think!"

He slid the barn door open and stepped outside.

CHAPTER 24

YOU HAVE TO GET YOUR HANDS DIRTY

GRIFFIN

Griffin watched the barn door slide back into place. He had bought Cheyenne some time, but in the long run—or even the short run—it wouldn't matter.

"Griffin? Griffin, is that you?" Cheyenne's voice was raw. "Please, you have to let me go."

"I can't." He started to explain, but her words crowded out his.

"You must really hate me, then." Her face contorted. "You lure me out here, and now you're just going to let them kill me?"

"Would you listen for a second? I'm handcuffed to a post, just like you. And until about five seconds ago, I had duct tape over my mouth."

"Wait—what?"

"All these months, I've left you alone, just like you wanted. But that doesn't mean I didn't think about you every day. Especially once I got to Portland and knew you were only a few miles away. I could have done what Dwayne did, figured out some way to contact you. But I didn't, because I was trying to keep my word, no matter how much I wanted to break it. I was doing what you *said* you wanted me to." Griffin's voice cracked, but he didn't care.

"But Dwayne said—"

"And you'll listen to him and not me? He was just messing with both of us, making you think I betrayed you, and driving me crazy since I was gagged and couldn't talk. I don't know what Dwayne told you in those messages, but it was him that wrote them, not me."

After a long pause, Cheyenne said, "He said you—or he or whatever—were going to kill yourself rather than testify against your dad." Her throat moved up and down as she swallowed. "And I couldn't let you do that."

"I'm not looking forward to testifying, but I would never kill myself over it." Maybe Griffin had flirted with the idea in his darker moments, but now he realized how much he wanted to live. He wanted to live so much. Too bad he was figuring that out when he was just about to die. "And what you said to TJ is right. I'm sure once he has the money, Dwayne's going to kill all of us. Even TJ. It's the one way he'll know for sure that we'll never testify."

"He won't kill you," Cheyenne said, but her voice wasn't as certain as her words. "You're Roy's only child."

"Yeah, but remember, my dad burned me and put me in the hospital for weeks when I was a kid. He killed my mom. Being related to Roy is not exactly a guarantee you'll be okay."

"But those were accidents."

Griffin couldn't believe Cheyenne was defending Roy. "Maybe my dad wouldn't kill me, but my uncle's not my dad. And he thinks I'm a traitor."

She lowered her voice. "Then we have to get out of here."

"I know that. But it's impossible."

"All I need is a thin piece of metal." Cheyenne walked her legs partway around the pole so that she was sitting at a different angle, and now he could see more clearly that her fingers were sweeping over the ground. "Like a piece of wire or a bobby pin, something like that."

"How will that help?"

"Because the lady who's been my bodyguard taught me how to get out of handcuffs. Wait"—her face lit up—"what do you have in your pockets?"

A flash of hope shot through him and then died. "Not much. Gum. My wallet. Maybe five bucks and some change." After a pause, he added a little reluctantly, "And a lighter. But no wire."

"Then look on the ground for something." She was still keeping her voice low. "It doesn't have to be very long. Even an inch might be enough."

"But it's dark. The flashlight's pointing at you. I can't see anything."

She made a raspberry sound. "That's what your hands are for. Make them be your eyes. That's how I can tell if I've wiped a counter off or swept the floor clean. I touch it. You have to get your hands dirty. Just make sure you overlap, so you don't miss anything."

Griffin remembered now how Cheyenne had been able to know things he didn't. It wasn't that she had super-human senses, but that having her eyes turned off allowed her to pay attention to what everyone else felt, touched, tasted, and smelled—and ignored.

As Griffin began to run his fingertips over the hard-beaten earth, Cheyenne said, "How did you end up here?"

"Dwayne threatened me after my mom's funeral. He said he'd have TJ hurt Aunt Debby if I didn't get in the van. So I got in. A little bit later, they handcuffed me and threw me in the back."

"Was Octavio's body back there then?" Cheyenne's voice broke when she said the man's name.

Griffin sighed. "Yeah. Only I didn't know who it was until later, when Dwayne told me. I just knew things were bad and going to get worse." Under his left ring finger, something rolled. It was thin, stiff, and a cylinder. His heart thrilled. But when he plucked it up and twisted his head, he saw it was yellow. Just a stiff piece of straw.

There had to be another way. Was there something

on him that wasn't in his pockets but still made of metal? No metal on the tips of the laces of his dress shoes. He still had a hole in one ear, but he hadn't worn an earring for a couple of years.

His belt!

"Cheyenne, my belt has a metal buckle," he whispered hoarsely. "Could you use that?"

Her voice changed. "Maybe? How thick is that part you put through the holes? As thick around as a bobby pin?"

He had to contort himself, the cuffs cutting into his wrists, until he could rest a finger on it. "No. It's pretty thick. Like three or four times that."

"That's too big." She took a breath. "Keep looking."

If he didn't have something on his clothes, maybe she did? "Don't some bras have, like, underwires in them?"

"They do, but I'm not wearing that kind."

It was hopeless. But what else could they do? Reaching back as far as he could, he trailed his fingers along the ground, slowly scooting around the post.

Just when Griffin was beginning to despair, he touched something right at the edge of where he could reach. He stopped breathing, concentrating on slowly scooting it in by curling his finger.

Finally he had it. "I've got something, Cheyenne. A piece of wire, about four inches long. And I think it's the right thickness."

"Can you toss it to me? Or by me?"

The seesaw of emotions continued as he contemplated how far away she was. "I don't see how. We're, like, twenty feet apart, and it's not like I can really swing my arm."

"What if you pushed yourself to your feet and tossed it high?"

He shook his head, forgetting again that she couldn't see him. "I think the chance that it would work is about zero. Can't you walk me through how to do it? And quick, before one of them comes back here?"

"I'll try. You just need to do it right once, then you'll be free and can bring me the wire. Okay, let me think. Is it flat or round? If it's round, you can make it act like a key. If it's flat, you can shim it between the teeth and the cuff."

He rolled it between his fingers to be sure. "It's round."

"Then we're making a key. Are you right-handed?"

"Yeah."

"First twist your wrists so they're nearly parallel and throw your elbows out to give yourself as much room as you can. Then you have to find the keyhole on your left cuff. It will be on one edge or the other, not in the middle. Be careful not to press the cuffs against anything, or they'll ratchet even tighter."

Griffin did as she said, sliding the tip of his right index finger over both sides of the cuff until he located a small hole. "Okay. I found the keyhole." The corner of the post was digging into his back, but he ignored the pain. His focus had narrowed to the tiny keyhole. If he could just do this, he could save them. That was all he asked, that they be allowed to live. Or at least that Cheyenne would.

"Now put just the tip of the wire into the keyhole and bend it over until the wire is parallel with the cuff."

"Which direction do I bend it?"

"That part doesn't matter. Handcuff keys aren't complicated. You're going to end up with a bend of about forty-five degrees, but the end piece is going to be really short, like a quarter of an inch long. You don't want it to be too long, or it won't fit into the keyhole right."

Gritting his teeth in concentration, Griffin put the tip of the wire in, pushed it down to bend it, pulled it out, and then traced it with his finger to see if it felt right. His palms and even the tips of his fingers were slick with sweat. He kept looking at the barn door, willing TJ to stay away.

"Okay, I've got it bent. I think it's right."

"Now stick it in the keyhole so that the long, straight piece of the wire runs from one side of your wrist to the other, right up the cuff. Then lift it up so that it moves straight back. When it's standing straight up from the cuff, slowly turn it away from your wrist. You're going to be angling that bent tip in toward the body of the cuff. And at some point, it's going to catch like the key would."

Griffin pictured it in his head. Even though he had

trouble reading, machines and mechanical things always made sense to him. Once he had taken apart his alarm clock to see how it worked. When he put it back together, he had had one tiny leftover plastic part, but the clock still told time.

Closing his eyes and holding his breath to help him concentrate, he put the wire back in the hole again, oriented the way Cheyenne had said. Slowly, he lifted it up until it was at about a ninety-degree angle to the cuff. He began to turn it.

And then he felt the piece of wire spring away into the darkness behind him.

Tears stung his eyes. He had failed her. Again. "I'm sorry, Cheyenne. It jumped out of my fingers when I was turning it."

"Just pick it up!" Her whisper was sharp with anxiety. "Try again!"

"I can't." He hated having to spell it out. "It was under so much tension it kind of flew. I heard it land, and it's way too far away."

"Just start looking again. If there was one piece of wire, there must be more. I'll keep looking, too." Then Cheyenne lifted her head. She sniffed hard. "Do you smell smoke?"

CHAPTER 25

COUNT ALL HER BONES

CHEYENNE

Cheyenne didn't need to hear Griffin swear to know that she was right. She did smell smoke. Something nearby was burning. She sniffed again, turning her face from side to side. The fire was on her left, closer to her than it was to Griffin.

When TJ knocked the cigarette from Dwayne's hand, it must have landed on some of the moldy hay. And instead of dying out, it had settled down and made itself at home. Now it was growing, and she could only sit and wait as it came for her.

She was going to die here, handcuffed to a post. She and Griffin both were. Die in this abandoned barn, unable to move as the flames licked their skin and then turned them into human torches. Her hand was still throbbing from a single cigarette burn. What would it be like to feel that times a hundred thousand? If she and Griffin were lucky, they would pass out from smoke inhalation before the fire reached them. She imagined the authorities raking the ashes, how they would count all her bones before sending them back to Danielle and Nick.

No! She couldn't die here. She wouldn't! But what could she do? How much time did they have? Cheyenne turned her head until she caught an orange flicker of it in the corner of her left eye. "How big is it?" she asked Griffin.

"It's still pretty small. Like less than a foot around. But there's plenty of old hay for it to burn. Try kicking all the stuff around you away. If you do, maybe it won't be able to get to you." She heard his feet start to scuff over the earth.

But fires made sparks, the way a maple tree dropped hundreds of helicopters in the hopes of spreading its seeds. Even if they managed to push away all the fuel around them, eventually a spark would land on their hair or pant legs or the posts they were chained to. And then they would burn to death.

Griffin made a noise, low in his throat. It sounded like a choked sob. He had spent weeks in a burn unit. Dying in a fire must be a regular feature of his nightmares. "I'm going to yell for TJ," he said. "Maybe he'll help us."

Or maybe he would let them burn as punishment for Cheyenne's biting him. And if he was here, she couldn't work on getting out of the cuffs. "No! Wait!" she said.

"Let me think for a second." Something Griffin had said earlier was echoing in her head.

"What are you doing, Cheyenne?" Griffin's voice broke. "At least try to kick the hay away."

Then it came to her. Her watch! She twisted her wrists behind her back. Her finger moved from the face—it was a little after four in the morning—to the band. It was made of rubber and, like Griffin's belt, it closed with a metal prong and buckle. Only much smaller. The prong was narrow, thin, mostly flat. But basically the right size. She just needed to flatten it a bit more if she wanted it to fit between the cuff and the rachet.

"Let me just try one more thing," she said, already unfastening the band.

"Hurry. The fire's starting to spread."

Holding one end of the watchband, Cheyenne twisted her head and her bound hands. She reached for the other end of the band with her open mouth. The handcuffs cut into her wrists, but still her jaws met only air. Pushing past the pain, she torqued her body, thrust her jaw forward, opened her mouth wide—and finally caught the buckle end between her front teeth. Hooking her tongue through the buckle, she inched it slowly back toward her molars. The band tasted of body lotion, and she resisted the urge to gag. Finally she maneuvered the prong between her back teeth and crushed them together. Then again. She just hoped they didn't crack before the prong flattened.

Then she reversed the whole process until the watchband was back in one hand. With the other, she ran her finger over the prong. It was now basically flat.

To shim a cuff, you had to slide in the shim and then press down on the cuff and the shim at the same time. Shimming was both easier and harder than picking cuffs. Easier because it didn't require as much skill. Harder because if you did it wrong, you would just end up with a cuff so tight it cut off the circulation to your hand.

Cheyenne was concentrating so intensely that even though she was starting to cough, she paid little attention to the smoke. Pressing her left cuff between her torso and the post to hold it still, she found the spot where the rachet disappeared into the cuff, and jimmied in the prong. When it felt seated, she said a silent prayer that mostly consisted of *Help me!* She pressed both the cuff and the prong in at the same time. The cuff tightened, beginning to cut into her wrist, but then she felt a tiny shift within it.

And when she twisted her left wrist, it opened.

She raised her hands—one free and one with a dangling cuff—over her head and shook them, both in triumph and to try to coax back the feeling.

"You did it." Griffin's whisper mingled excitement and fear. "Now get me out. And hurry!"

When Cheyenne pushed herself to her feet, the muscles in her thighs and calves cramped. She felt like a wooden doll come to clumsy life. Moving in the direction of Griffin's voice, she didn't even take time to pull out her cane. Instead she folded her right arm across her belly like a bumper and swung her left arm like a feeler. The space seemed as empty as it felt and sounded. In nine strides, her outstretched hand hit the post Griffin was chained to. She fell to her knees, groping for his cuffs.

"Hurry," he urged. "Oh God, please, Cheyenne, hurry."

"Cheyenne!" TJ yelled from outside. "Hang on, Cheyenne. I'm coming!" The barn door rattled and squealed as he began to slide it back open.

Adrenaline shot through her veins. Where could she go? What could she do? TJ on one side, the fire on the other, and Griffin trapped in the middle.

"Follow my lead," she said into Griffin's ear, and then she hurried the nine steps back to her post, sat down, and put her hands—one cuffed and one not—behind her back.

"Help me! TJ! Put out the fire!" It was crackling hungrily now. Cheyenne let her panic show in her voice.

She heard him rush past her, then his big boots stamping over and over as he coughed. When she turned her head back and forth, the orange flickers were gone. The smoke was now so thick it felt like cotton in her lungs.

"Thank you so much for saving me." Cheyenne needed to coax him closer. If she made the first move, he would see it coming and it would be over before it began.

"I shouldn't have." His tone was petulant. "Not after you bit me."

"I was just scared." She made her voice soft and meek. "I'm sorry."

TJ's only answer was a grunt.

"My wrists are hurting me. I can't feel my hands. Please, can you help me?"

"I'm supposed to leave you alone, remember?" he said sullenly.

"I'm sure Dwayne didn't mean you should let my hands die from lack of circulation."

"I don't have the key." She heard him turn and start to walk away.

"Please, TJ, please. I'm sorry. I shouldn't have bit you. I wasn't thinking." She made her voice break. "Can you just look at my wrists? Maybe you could move the hand-cuffs to a different spot or something."

He made an annoyed growl. "I guess." She heard him start back toward her. He sounded like he was about six feet away. She turned her head, trying to see him. Held her breath, trying to hear him. And when it felt like he was only a few inches away, she launched herself forward, sweeping her arms along the ground as if she was pull-ing his feet in for a hug. Her palms grabbed the backs of his heels just as her shoulder found his knees and drove forward.

TJ yelled as he fell, landing so hard she actually heard

something crack. Keeping hold of his legs, she scrambled up to sit on his chest, her knees on either side and high into his armpits so that he couldn't buck her off.

Cheyenne pulled her right fist back. Her fingers were wrapped around the empty handcuff so it was like a set of brass knuckles. And then she hit TJ's temple as hard as she could.

And felt him go limp.

CHAPTER 26

CAREFUL WHAT YOU ASK FOR

CHEYENNE

"You did it, Cheyenne!" Griffin shouted. "You knocked him out! I can't believe you did that."

"Sorry. It was just automatic." Cheyenne felt a little sick at how quickly she had reacted. Thinking hadn't even really entered into it. All those months training with Jaydra must have rewired her brain.

"No," Griffin clarified, "what I meant was, that was kind of amazing."

Cheyenne barely heard him. Her stomach dropped. TJ wasn't moving. Was he dead? She gave his shoulder a shake, and he let out a huffing sound, but nothing more. She gingerly touched his temple with the fingers of her empty left hand. It was slick with blood. She pressed a little harder, sliding her fingers in a circle. If she had broken his skull, it wasn't obvious. Which was a relief.

"He's still breathing," she said.

"Right now I'm not sure I would care if he wasn't." Griffin said. "Where'd you learn to do that?"

"Jaydra's been teaching me self-defense."

"Jaydra?"

Cheyenne remembered that it was really Dwayne, not Griffin, who knew about Jaydra. "My bodyguard. The same one who taught me how to get out of handcuffs."

"Whoever she is, she did a great job. And speaking of handcuffs, hurry and get mine off. We need to get out of here before Dwayne gets back."

Cheyenne got to her feet. Reaching into her coat pocket, she pulled out her cane and shook it. The clack of the rods snapping into place had never sounded so good. With a cane, her strides were longer, so instead of counting steps, she walked in the direction of Griffin's voice until her cane tapped his leg. She went to her knees. The watch was still on the ground behind him where she had dropped it. In a few seconds, his cuffs were off.

"Before we leave, we'd better lock up TJ." She shimmed off her own remaining handcuff, the one she had used as a weapon.

They each took an arm and dragged TJ to the post that had been Cheyenne's just a few minutes earlier. The metallic smell of his blood made her stomach rebel.

"How badly do you think I hurt him?" She pulled his hands back, and Griffin fastened them together with the cuffs that had seconds earlier been on her wrists.

"I think you just knocked him out. Nothing permanent."

"But what if he doesn't wake up?" She remembered the cracking sound when he fell. Maybe he was in some kind of coma.

"You only did what you had to do," Griffin said. "Besides, he's probably okay. I mean, he's still breathing."

"But I can hear blood dripping on the floor."

"Head wounds always bleed a lot." Griffin's tone didn't sound as confident as his words.

They both jumped when TJ let out a long, low groan. Cheyenne grabbed Griffin's arm. "Okay, let's get out of here."

"Wait a sec," Griffin said. "TJ might have a phone. If we call the police, maybe they could get here before Dwayne does." Cheyenne heard the sounds of hands sliding over cloth, another groan as Griffin shifted TJ. "Here it is, in his back pocket." A pause. "Oh."

"What?"

"It's completely smashed," Griffin said. "I can't even get it to power up. It must be from when you knocked him over."

So that was the cracking sound she had heard. "Then I guess we just go. But where?"

Griffin put his lips next to her ear. She shivered at the touch of his breath. "Just in case TJ's more awake than he looks, let's go over by the barn door where he can't hear us." He took her left arm. Her cane was still in her right hand, and she let it trail behind her. As they got near the sliding door, the air became fresher. After Griffin slid the squealing door open a little farther, she stepped outside, leaned against the wall to steady herself, and took grateful gulps of the clean-smelling air.

"I guess we'll have to run," he said in a low voice, "but I'm not sure how far we'll get."

"Don't worry, I can keep up." In PE, Cheyenne ran with a partner, both of them holding a strip of old towel, and she was pretty fast.

"That's not it." Griffin sighed. "You can't see where we are, but I did last night. There's only one road and nothing else but flat fields. And whatever is growing in them is not that tall, so if we try to cut across, Dwayne will see us a mile away."

She imagined Dwayne pushing the accelerator down, the van bouncing over furrows until it hit them and threw them high in the air.

"We don't have any choice, though, do we? We just go and hope someone else drives down the road before he does or that we make it someplace before he gets to us." Cheyenne caned a few feet farther, then turned in a circle.

"Is the sun rising?" Her watch said it was about four thirty, and it seemed to her that in one direction the sky was lightening.

"Yeah. It's just starting to get light."

Just orienting herself using cardinal directions made Cheyenne feel better. She pointed with her cane. "Let's go that way. North. That should be toward Portland."

Instead of answering, Griffin swore. "I see headlights. I think it's Dwayne coming back."

She thought of Octavio, of the bullet hole in his chest. Would she and Griffin soon be lying dead in the back of the van next to him? Where could they go? What could they do? If they tried to leave now, Dwayne would surely see them.

"There's another door around the corner." Griffin grabbed her arm. "It seems like a separate space. Maybe we can hide there and Dwayne will think we've left—and then we really can leave after he goes looking for us."

After yanking the barn's sliding door closed, he hurried her around the corner, then opened what sounded like a regular door. Inside, the air was thick with the smell of mildew.

"There's a stack of old hay, like three or four bales deep and taller than our heads," Griffin said. "I think we can squeeze behind it."

It didn't seem like the best choice, but there weren't any others. As Cheyenne folded up her cane, she heard Griffin suck in his breath. He leaned down and picked something up. "We got lucky," he said. "Someone left a hay hook behind. " He took her hand and put her fingers on it. She traced its shape. It had an open metal handle shaped like a rectangle. The handle was fastened to a long shaft of metal that ended in a curve with a wicked point. It made her think of Captain Hook.

He took her hand again, and she followed him as they wriggled themselves between the scratchy hay and the rough wooden wall. As the hay poked her cheeks, got caught in her hair, and snagged her clothes, Cheyenne prayed she wouldn't sneeze or cough from the dust and mold. Even the smell of smoke seemed stronger in here.

They had gone only a few feet when they froze at the sound of an engine. She hoped it would fade away, but instead it came closer and closer before stopping in front of the barn, the engine idling.

Dwayne was nearly back. Cheyenne's heart was slamming in her chest.

He got out, his feet crunching on the gravel. The barn door screeched open, and then Dwayne drove in. He was already shouting as he turned off the engine and jumped out.

"TJ! What happened!"

Cheyenne didn't hear any answer. Evidently, Dwayne didn't either, because the next sound was the thud of a kick, followed by TJ groaning.

"What happened? Did they set some kind of fire? And Griffin must've had a handcuff key on him. I guess he really does take after his dad." The grudging admiration in Dwayne's voice turned to annoyance. "Wake up, idiot! Tell me when they left. Tell me which way they went."

Dwayne was so busy yelling that he didn't notice the sound of a second vehicle pulling up to the barn. But Cheyenne did. Griffin must have, too, because he squeezed her wrist.

The engine of the second vehicle turned off. A door opened, and feet stepped out onto the gravel. The next thing Cheyenne heard was the most welcome sound in the world. Jaydra's voice.

"Hold it right there! Put your hands over your head!"

Dwayne didn't answer.

"Show me your hands!" Jaydra shouted. "I need to see your hands!"

"Okeydokey." Dwayne's tone was loose, unhurried. "Here you go."

A shot split the world in two. Jaydra grunted.

Cheyenne put her hand over her mouth to stifle a scream. She heard Jaydra take one step on the gravel, then another, and then fall to the ground.

And Dwayne said, "Hey, you asked to see my hands. Didn't anyone ever tell you to be careful what you ask for?"

CHAPTER 27

TOO LATE FOR YOU

CHEYENNE

The last sound Jaydra had made before she collapsed on the gravel was a grunt. Now even though Cheyenne strained her ears, outside the barn it was deathly quiet. Not a moan, not a whisper.

Her blood turned to slush. *No,* she thought. *No, please, God. Please let her be alive.*

Already starting to move from behind the stacked hay bales, she whispered to Griffin, "We have to help Jaydra."

Griffin grabbed her arm. "We can't," he said next to her ear. "If we go out there, Dwayne will shoot us, too."

"But we just can't leave her," Cheyenne said in a strangled whisper. "She'll die." What she didn't say, what neither of them said, was that Jaydra might already be dead.

It was Dwayne who got to Jaydra first. Cheyenne bit

her lip as she heard one foot scuff through the gravel and then connect solidly with flesh as he kicked her.

Jaydra moaned in response. She was alive!

"Don't think you'll be needing this anymore." Dwayne's voice was muffled. He must have been bending down, taking Jaydra's gun. That meant Dwayne now had two guns and everyone else had none.

When Jaydra spoke, her voice was pinched with pain. Cheyenne had to strain to hear her. "The police are right behind me."

"Maybe, baby." Dwayne spoke without urgency. "But whichever way it is, I think they'll be too late for you."

Jaydra had told Cheyenne that she would die for her, and Cheyenne had just rolled her eyes. Now Cheyenne was letting her die alone in the dirt. There had to be something she could do before it was too late. Before what Dwayne had said came true.

"We have to help her," she insisted in an urgent whisper.

"Wait until he leaves," Griffin whispered back. "As soon as he goes to try to find us, then we can."

Dwayne's footsteps crunched. "I do appreciate the ride, though. It's a lot sweeter than that van." Cheyenne waited for him to get inside Jaydra's car, but instead he said, "My, my, what do we have here?"

To her horror, the footsteps came closer. Then the

door to their hiding place creaked open. Both she and Griffin froze, not even breathing.

In a lilting voice, Dwayne said, "Come out, come out wherever you are."

Neither of them moved.

"I can see part of your white cane, Cheyenne. No sense in pretending you're not there. Suck it up, buttercup. Come on out before I put a bullet hole in you, the way I have all your friends."

What choice did she have? Cheyenne began to edge her way out from behind the hay bales.

Behind her, she felt Griffin shift as he took his hand off her and put it on the hay hook. She reached back and pressed down on the tool, signaling that he should drop it. He didn't. In her mind, Cheyenne yelled at him to leave it. If Dwayne felt threatened, she had no doubt that he would shoot Griffin. Half nephew or no half nephew.

"Good thing you're still here, Cheyenne," Dwayne said, "or I would be in a very bad mood. And just when things were looking up. Your father should be wiring us the Bitcoins right about now." He sniffed. "Who's a lucky duck? Smells like that fire didn't get put out all the way. Well, I say burn, baby, burn."

Cheyenne had been concentrating so hard on hiding that she hadn't noticed the pall of smoke was getting worse. TJ must not have stamped the fire all the way out.

Now he was handcuffed next to the place where it had started.

She slid free of the hay bales. Bits of straw stuck to her hair and sweaty skin.

"Okay, Griffin, now you too," Dwayne said. "And stay loosey-goosey."

Cheyenne heard Griffin suck in a breath, as if he was readying himself to make a move. What was he going to try to do? The hay hook was an ugly tool, but it would be no match for a gun.

Dwayne took a step forward, and she felt something hard press into the flesh of her forehead. "And just so you don't get any ideas, the gun is now resting right between your little friend's eyes."

She had to do something before it was too late. She and Jaydra had practiced so many ways Cheyenne could defend herself with her cane, but the scenarios had all been theoretical. She had gone through the motions, never believing she would have to use them. Now their lives depended on something working in real life.

Praying that the gun in Dwayne's hand made him feel invincible, Cheyenne stepped forward on her left foot, cutting an angle so that Dwayne was no longer directly in front of her. As she did, she swung her folded cane across her body in a big circle, striking his wrist and pushing the gun past her.

A bullet sang past her ear and buried itself in the

wooden wall. Dwayne cursed as the gun flew from his hand and thudded onto the packed dirt.

Cheyenne wanted to freeze, to contemplate how close death had just come. But in her head, she heard Jaydra's voice urging her to keep moving.

With her left hand, Cheyenne grabbed for Dwayne's shoulder. At first she found only air. *No, no, no.* She pawed the air again, more desperately, and this time the palm of her hand met the top of his shoulder. She pushed down hard, pivoting at the same time, and kicked the back of his knee. Off balance from being pushed in two directions, Dwayne fell to one knee. Just as she swung her folded cane at his face as hard as she could.

It smashed flesh and bone. Hot blood spattered her fingers as Dwayne let out a scream. She felt him reaching out, presumably for the gun. If he got it, he would take only a second to finish what he had started. She couldn't let that happen.

She slipped behind him, wrapping her right arm around his thick throat. It was like trying to throttle a bull. She needed to put pressure on his carotid arteries to cut off the blood supply to his brain. To give herself extra leverage, she tucked the folded cane in her right hand on the far side of her head. Her neck held it in place, so that her arm tightened around his throat like a vise.

"What are you doing?" Griffin sounded equal parts scared and awed. "Do you need help?"

Dwayne's hands clawed at her forearm. But his nails were short, and he couldn't get any purchase. She pressed her cheek against his shoulder blade to lessen the chance that he could hit her.

"I'm okay," she panted. "Get his gun."

As Griffin scrabbled for it, Dwayne squirmed and struggled, finally silent as the depth of his predicament became clear to him and his supply of oxygen began to dwindle. Full of adrenaline, Cheyenne hit him with her left hand, once in the ribs and twice in the temple. She wished she still had the cuffs to serve as brass knuckles. In theory, it should take less than ten seconds for him to lose consciousness.

It had always been imaginary when she had practiced it with Jaydra. Now it was real. It was real, and Jaydra was dying.

Finally, just as Cheyenne's arm was beginning to tremble, she felt Dwayne's body go limp. She held on for a few more seconds and then released the cane and let him go. He landed like a two-hundred-pound bag of flour.

"Quick," Cheyenne told Griffin, "put some handcuffs on him. He won't be unconscious for long."

At least she hoped he wouldn't. Had she held the choke for too long or not long enough?

Griffin retrieved the second gun from Dwayne's waistband. Since this room didn't have any handy posts, they settled for cuffing his hands behind him and rolling him onto his back. Griffin took the handcuff key from Dwayne's pocket and threw it behind the hay.

As they manhandled him, Dwayne seemed completely limp. Was he even breathing? Cheyenne wasn't willing to put her face right above his, to feel and listen for his breath. Instead she put her hand over his mouth, the way she had with Octavio. Only this time she felt warm air puff out of his nose. She let out a breath she didn't know she had been holding. He was alive.

Then he made a rattling sound like a snore on steroids. It was crazy loud, but he still didn't stir. He did it again.

Dwayne was obviously breathing, but it didn't sound like normal breathing. It made her think of hibernating bears or World War I biplanes. Had she crushed his windpipe? Cheyenne put her hands on his shoulders. To her horror, she felt his whole body begin to shake. Was he having a seizure? Had she cut off the oxygen too long, damaged his brain?

But then things got even worse.

Because TJ started screaming from the barn. "I'm on fire! I'm on fire!"

CHAPTER 28

PLEAD, PRAY, MOAN, AND SOMETIMES SCREAM

GRIFFIN

Griffin froze, a cold fist of horror replacing his heart.

He remembered screaming like TJ was when he was ten.

His dad had been out in the barn, which was only a little less dilapidated than this one, "cooking." Griffin had been too young to understand that didn't mean food, but meth. That day, he had been playing with one of the stray kittens in the yard when it suddenly raced away from him. He gave chase, running after it into the barn.

Roy hadn't heard Griffin run up behind him and had startled. The meth had blazed up, catching Griffin's shirt on fire.

At first it hadn't even felt hot. It had been like he was wearing a tie made of the coldest ice cubes in the universe. Then suddenly it *was* hot, red hot, eating through him. Griffin had managed to rip off his shirt as his dad swore and batted at the flames, or he would have been burned even worse. He had wanted to die or pass out, but managed to do neither. Not in the barn, not in the ambulance, not in the hospital.

He'd spent weeks in the burn unit, listening to other survivors plead, pray, moan, and sometimes scream. People said it was the lucky ones who cried from the pain, because if you didn't, it meant your nerves had been burned away.

Now Griffin hated fire in every form. He hated candles, gas stoves, campfires, even his own lighter. Once when he was angry at himself, at how he looked, angry at the sidelong looks his red ribbons of scars earned him, he went inside a bathroom stall at school and locked it behind him. Then he had flicked his lighter and held out the flame, run his palm over it until his mind cleared of everything but pain.

TJ screamed again, waking Griffin out of his trance. "I've got to try to help him, Cheyenne," he said.

Even as she begged him not to go, he grabbed up the hay hook and ran out of the storage area and around the corner of the barn. Next to a Cadillac Escalade parked in front of the open sliding door lay a young woman with a long black braid, her upper body in a dark puddle. She had propped herself up on her elbows, but her face was pale as the moon, shiny with sweat. Past her, past the open barn door, past the white van parked inside, the back of the barn was fully engulfed in fire. TJ was silhouetted against the crackling orange flames. He had managed to push himself to his feet, his hands still locked behind him around the post.

He screamed again, but now it wasn't even words, just a long, high-pitched howl. But TJ wasn't on fire. Not yet.

The wooden post he was handcuffed to had begun to burn at the base. TJ's feet danced as he tried to avoid the flames that were climbing higher.

Griffin sprinted toward him, not even thinking that he had never liked TJ and that he didn't have a handcuff key or anything to fight the fire. It felt as if he were being given a chance to save himself on that terrible day nearly eight years ago.

Holding the hay hook, Griffin leaped over a small pocket of fire that separated him from TJ. The heart of the blaze was farther back, where Dwayne's cigarette must have landed. Wishing for his lace-up boots, Griffin kicked at the flames at the base of the post with his flimsy and ineffectual dress shoes. If only he hadn't thrown away the key.

Maybe he could break down the post with the hay hook. "Move your feet as far out as you can," Griffin told TJ, "and then stay still."

TJ continued to caper, too lost in fear to listen, blood gleaming on the side of his face where Cheyenne had hit him. Ducking, Griffin pushed one shoulder against TJ's back to force him out of the way. He bent over and began to hack at the post with the sharp hook. The handle was only wide enough for one hand, so he wrapped his other hand underneath, at the top of the metal shaft.

His first strike gouged only a tiny dent, less than a half inch deep. He tried again, aiming the hook into the heart of the flames. And again. And again. It was hard to tell if he was making progress, but each strike of the hay hook felt like it landed a tiny bit deeper, and each time he had to pull a little harder to yank it free.

After about a dozen strikes, Griffin was tugging the hook free when flames suddenly began to race up the sleeve of his suit jacket. For a second he froze, ten years old again, terror lodged in his gut like a cannonball. Then he swatted the sleeve against his own leg until he killed the flames. Tearing off the still-smoking jacket, he threw it away from him, far back into the fire. It was consumed in seconds.

The pause made him come to his senses. What was he doing? It was a fool's errand to try to save anyone, and this was TJ. Besides, he wasn't getting anyplace. Long before he finished, the fire would eat both of them up and then probably finish off Jaydra for dessert.

If he left now, he could still save himself and help Cheyenne drag Jaydra farther away.

Without a word to TJ, Griffin sprinted for the barn door. He ran past the van and outside into the clean air.

Cheyenne was on her knees, pressing her hand against Jaydra's side while speaking in a low voice.

Griffin stopped a few feet away and dropped the hay hook, panting and coughing. Bracing his hands on his knees, he threw up.

CHAPTER 29

INTO THE INFERNO

CHEYENNE

After Griffin ran out of the storage area to help TJ, Cheyenne unfurled her cane and hurried after him, searching for Jaydra.

First her cane found the car Jaydra had driven. Cheyenne ran her hand along its side. Her fingers recognized the scratch she had accidentally made with Phantom's harness when she first got him. It was Danielle's Escalade. On the other side of the Escalade, guided by the sound of breathing that sounded all wrong, she found Jaydra.

She fell to her knees. "Are you okay?" Already knowing the answer was no.

In the barn behind her, Griffin was yelling at TJ, telling him to move away from the post. TJ was still screaming, but now he wasn't even using words.

"Are you okay?" Jaydra asked her own question instead of answering Cheyenne's. "I heard a gunshot."

"It didn't hit anybody. It happened when I disarmed the guy who shot you. Dwayne. He's Roy's brother. And then I choked him out with my cane, just like we practiced. Griffin helped me handcuff him." In just the few seconds she had been by Jaydra's side, the fire seemed to have gotten hotter. How fast was it spreading? Or maybe she should be worrying about what Dwayne would do once he regained consciousness. Cheyenne decided she would think about those things in a minute. Right now her priority was helping Jaydra.

"Way to go," Jaydra wheezed. "Good job."

"I had a good teacher." Cheyenne had to swallow back tears. "How bad are you hurt?"

For the second time, Jaydra ignored the question. Instead she said, "My phone's in my back pocket. Call 9-1-1."

Cheyenne pulled the phone free. Even though she tried to be gentle, Jaydra hissed in pain. She held the phone out so Jaydra could dial, then put it to her ear.

"Nine-one-one operator," a woman said briskly. "Police, fire, or medical?"

What should she answer? Around the corner, Dwayne was unconscious, handcuffed, and maybe brain damaged.

Griffin and TJ were caught in the flames crackling behind her. And in front of her, Jaydra lay bleeding from a gunshot wound.

"All of them!" she panted. "Police, fire and an ambulance. And hurry!"

"What's the address?"

I don't know where I am, she wanted to scream. "Can't you tell that from my phone?"

"It looks like you're on a cell phone in a rural location, so it will take us a bit to triangulate. Can you give us any clues to narrow it down? A landmark? A nearby business?"

"I think we're somewhere south of Portland." She remembered what Griffin had said. "There's nothing but fields around us. We're in front of an abandoned barn or stable or something. And right now, it's on fire!" The heat pressed against her back like a giant's flat hand. "I don't know the name of the road it's on."

Jaydra murmured something. Cheyenne leaned closer, putting one hand out to steady herself. It landed in a shallow warm pool. A pool of blood.

"Ralston," Jaydra said, and then coughed. "Ralston Road."

"Ralston Road," Cheyenne repeated frantically to the operator. "I've been kidnapped! And there's a woman who tried to help me, but she got shot. And she's bleeding a lot. So you need to hurry!"

The operator's voice was not quite so neutral now. "Where's the kidnapper?"

"There's two of them. And they're tied up in the burning barn."

"And what's your name?"

A spark landed on the back of her hand. Biting back a shriek, she shook it off her hand, then said, "Cheyenne Wilder."

"How old are you, honey?"

"Almost seventeen." The fire sounded louder now. The flat hand on her back had changed to a giant iron.

"Okay, I need you to stay on the line with me until the police get there."

"I can't. She's bleeding. I need to have both hands to help her."

"Then put the phone on the ground, but don't disconnect. We've got units headed your way, but they're a few minutes out."

Cheyenne did as the dispatcher instructed, then leaned over Jaydra. "They've got people coming, but it feels like you're bleeding a lot. How can I stop it?"

"Find the entrance wound." Jaydra had to pause between words. "On my left side."

Thinking of Octavio, Cheyenne slipped her fingers under Jaydra's T-shirt. She found a hole about a half inch across on the left side of her ribs. Under her fingertips, blood bubbled. "Should I put pressure on it?"

"Not yet. See if"—Jaydra moaned, and Cheyenne reflexively lifted her hand—"if you can find an exit wound."

Gingerly, Cheyenne began to pat the far side of Jaydra's torso with her other hand.

Jaydra swore. "Just stick your hand up my shirt. Wipe it over my skin and feel for blood."

Cheyenne obeyed. Jaydra's torso was slick, but when Cheyenne rubbed her fingers together, they weren't tacky. It was just sweat, a lot of sweat, but not blood. "I can't find an exit wound."

"Good. One less hole to worry about. Ball up the bottom of my shirt and press it against the hole." When she did, Jaydra gasped in pain. Cheyenne started to pull back, but Jaydra rasped out, "Keep pressing." Her breaths sounded more like groans.

Both of them were also starting to cough. The air felt thick. Cheyenne's eyes were watering, and she tasted ashes on her tongue. "How come you didn't bring the cops with you?" she asked, then hoped it didn't sound like an accusation.

"Your dad thought you went on a joyride. He didn't want to get the cops involved." Jaydra paused to cough. "We thought it'd work better if it was just one of us at first, not a posse. So I came. I could see your location, and when it started deviating from where the car was, I thought you might be hitchhiking. I didn't let them know, because I wasn't sure. Of course, none of us expected this."

"I thought I was coming to help Griffin, but Dwayne, that guy who shot you, was pretending to be him." Cheyenne ran Jaydra's words back through her mind. "What do you mean, you could see my location? How did you know where I was?"

"Your new cane. I modified it. It has a GPS tracker inside."

The same cane that had allowed her to turn the tables on Dwayne. Cheyenne said, "So I guess it saved me twice."

Someone ran out of the barn. It was Griffin, coughing, choking, struggling to breathe. He dropped something on the ground. It was followed seconds later by the sound of vomit splattering. He gagged and heaved.

"Griffin!" TJ howled from the barn. "Don't leave me! Please! I can't die like this!"

Griffin took a long, shaky breath. Then Cheyenne heard him say to himself, "TJ's right. Come on, Griff. Let's do this."

"No!" she shouted. "Griffin, don't!"

But then she heard him run back into the inferno.

CHAPTER 30

CAN'T DIE LIKE THIS

GRIFFIN

"Griffin!" TJ howled from deep inside the barn. "Help me! Please! I can't die like this!"

Griffin reminded himself that it was TJ who was begging him. The guy he had had to pull off Cheyenne six months earlier. The guy who had shot Jimbo, who was supposedly his friend, and not even blinked. TJ did not possess a single redeeming quality.

But even though it was TJ, Griffin knew that the other man was right. No one deserved to die like he would if Griffin left him there. Griffin could imagine what it would be like. He could imagine it better than anyone. The stench of your own flesh burning. The pain flaying you, electric and sharp and inescapable as you begged to die. But you wouldn't. At least not fast enough.

It was probably suicide to go back in there, but Griffin didn't think he could live with himself if he just let TJ burn to death. He picked up the hay hook and ran back into the barn. The smoke had gotten even thicker, the pockets of fire bigger. Behind him, Cheyenne was yelling, begging him not to go, but he ignored her. He couldn't afford to pay attention to her or to think about what he was doing, or he'd never do it.

TJ was now standing as far from the burning post as he could, given that he was handcuffed to it. His arms were so far up and back that he had to be in danger of dislocating his shoulders. The fire was only inches from his linked wrists. TJ's lips were moving, but Griffin couldn't hear anything he said. He might have been praying. His eyes were so wide that there was white on either side.

Behind TJ, the fire was mesmerizing. Red, orange, and yellow flames danced and intertwined. The fire was alive and breathing.

Griffin tore his gaze away. Skidding to a stop next to the post, he set his feet. Hefting the hay hook over one shoulder, he took a deep breath, twisted his hips, and swung as hard as he could at the spot he had attacked earlier, about a foot off the ground. This time the hook lodged in the burning wood and he could not shake it free. He yanked with all his might. Beside him, TJ grunted as he used his handcuffs to pull at the beam.

Above them the roof began to groan. Griffin blinked away the smoke, struggling to focus. The post was definitely starting to bend. With a huge yank, he finally managed to pull the hay hook free. He immediately struck again, even more fiercely, ignoring how the metal had heated up and was searing his fingers. Both he and TJ were now coughing nonstop. Griffin's tongue was a piece of leather in his mouth.

The flames flanked them. The two of them worked at the post in silence, past words, past thought, breathing ash, surrounded by the roar of the fire consuming everything in its path.

And then suddenly the post sagged as it cracked lengthwise. Giant splinters exploded into the air, narrowly missing them. Feeling a fresh surge of adrenaline, Griffin gave it a half dozen more blows and broke it all the way through.

TJ squatted and yanked his handcuffs through the gap. Griffin looked down. TJ's hair was on fire. He slapped at it with his free hand. TJ looked confused for a second before he realized what was happening. And then Griffin grabbed TJ's elbow, and together the two of them raced out of the barn.

Outside, Cheyenne had managed to drag Jaydra behind the Escalade, putting its bulk between the injured woman and the fire. Jaydra's heels had left two furrows in the gravel, with a shiny trail of dark blood in the middle.

Coughing, TJ staggered toward the road. But Griffin

had eyes only for Cheyenne—and her attention was focused on Jaydra. He dropped to his knees on the damp ground beside them. The sky had lightened enough that he could see Jaydra's face. He wondered if the fire was making his eyes play tricks on him, because her lips were a strange color, a pale purple.

"We already called 9-1-1," Cheyenne said. "They said help is coming."

Jaydra's head lolled in what might have been a shake. "Not soon enough." She coughed, and suddenly blood was on her lips, outlining each of her teeth.

"I'll drive you to a hospital." Griffin said, praying one was close enough.

"Too late for that too." With a hiss, she raised her black T-shirt to expose her left side. It was so sodden with blood that it left her palm painted scarlet. "Tell me what you see." She gasped between words.

"There's a hole," Griffin said. "Like the size of a penny. And it's, um, bubbling." Nausea roiled through him. Blood bubbled out with each of her breaths. That couldn't be right.

"It's a"—the cords stood out on Jaydra's neck as she struggled to breathe—"sucking chest wound. You have to . . . put something over it . . . to keep air out. . . . Like a candy wrapper. . . . Then tie . . . in place."

Griffin saw that when Jaydra breathed in, only the

right side of her chest rose. Just one lung must have been working, which probably meant there wasn't enough oxygen in her blood.

Once more, he took mental inventory of his pockets. "I don't have anything like that." He was ready to jump to his feet, start scouring the roadside ditch for any piece of trash. TJ was on his hands and knees next to the ditch, gagging and coughing.

But Cheyenne was already scrabbling in her raincoat. She pulled out a green plastic bag with a picture of a cartoon dog on it. "Don't worry, it's never been used."

Jaydra didn't react to Cheyenne's words. She seemed to be focused internally. As if, Griffin thought, she was ordering herself not to die.

"Take off . . . my shirt. . . . Make bandage."

Griffin helped Cheyenne maneuver Jaydra like a doll, pulling the T-shirt over each arm and then her head. One side of her white bra was soaked in blood.

Something big crashed to the ground behind them. Griffin turned. The back wall of the barn had collapsed in an explosion of sparks. He didn't think they were in any immediate danger, but he was glad they were sheltered by the Escalade. Even with the SUV between them and the fire, the temperature had to be close to 120 degrees.

Jaydra touched him with a cold hand, and he turned back. Her skin looked like wax. "Have to force . . . air out. When I nod . . . put bag on."

Griffin took the plastic bag. She exhaled forcefully. He watched with horror as a bubble as big as a half-dollar was pushed out of the wound. He could hear air coming out of both her mouth and the bullet hole. Jaydra nodded, and he slapped the plastic bag flat and then held it in place. It moved slightly under his palm as she inhaled.

Cheyenne was trying to tear the T-shirt into strips. She put her fingers in the bullet hole of the shirt and pulled, but the T-shirt didn't tear. She put the hole to her mouth and grabbed it with her teeth, with no more effect. Blood rimmed her mouth, making her look like a vampire.

Jaydra's lips moved, but Griffin had to put his ear against her mouth to hear. "On my calf . . . knife."

He checked with his free hand and found a holster. As he slid the knife free, he wondered where her purse was and what she carried in it. A tiny nuclear warhead?

He had Cheyenne put her hand on the bag while he set to work on the T-shirt with the six-inch-long knife. With a feeling of triumph, he finally managed to saw a strip from the bottom. He pushed it under Jaydra's torso and then grabbed it from underneath. But the T-shirt, which had gone around Jaydra without much room to spare, was not nearly long enough to be tied in place over the bandage.

Jaydra's lips moved again, but now there was no sound behind them. Griffin thought she said, "Hurry."

"I'll have to cut some more strips and tie them together."

As he frantically sawed at the wet fabric, he heard sirens. Relief washed over him. An ambulance would have real supplies, not an empty dog poop bag and bloody strips of torn T-shirt.

But when he looked up, Griffin saw only two cop cars speeding up the road. No ambulance. No firetruck. He didn't stop hacking at the T-shirt. Jaydra's eyes were only half open, her head slumped to one side. She must be unconscious.

He wouldn't let himself think that she might be dead.

Less than a minute later, the two squad cars skidded to a stop about thirty feet away from them. The cops were out in a second, both of them shouting, their words overlapping as they crouched and drew their guns from behind the protection of their open doors.

"Drop the weapon! Drop your weapon now!"

Weapon? Who were they talking to?

The cops caught Griffin's eye. He swore. He had forgotten all about Dwayne. He must have regained consciousness and then managed to slip his cuffs in front of him. Now he was creeping up behind one of the cops, a youngish guy with a strong nose and ears that stuck out from the side of his head.

The cop's narrow eyes were fixed on Griffin. "Drop your weapon!" he shouted again, and the other cop echoed him.

Griffin got to his feet and shouted, pointing with the knife. "Watch out! Dwayne's behind you!"

"Drop your weapon!" the first cop yelled again, his gaze never wavering from Griffin.

"Drop it now!" the second cop shouted.

Griffin realized the cops were looking only at him. That they were shouting at him.

And, a second later, they were shooting at him.

CHAPTER 31

BLOOD EVERYWHERE

TJ

After he finished getting sick in the ditch at the edge of the road, TJ straightened up. Getting free of the fire had left his mind just as empty as his belly now was. His hair was singed, his skin pockmarked with burns, his hands still cuffed behind him.

He looked around blankly. The sun was just beginning to rise. Two of the walls of the barn had collapsed, and the other two were sagging. Inside what remained, the van was burning, thick black smoke billowing from it. The recent rains and the fact that the barn was surrounded by gravel had kept the fire from spreading farther.

TJ began to stagger back to Cheyenne, who was sheltering at the back end of the Escalade. He moved toward her, even though it also meant moving closer to the fire, which was beginning to nibble at the SUV's front bumper.

He didn't know what he wanted anymore, but Cheyenne was still a touchstone, a reminder of the dreams that had kept him sane for months.

The woman Dwayne had shot lay dead on the ground in front of Cheyenne and Griffin. As he got closer, TJ saw there was blood everywhere. Blood on Cheyenne's lips and hands. Blood on Griffin's hands. Blood on the gravel. Blood on the dead woman's half-naked torso and trickling from her lips.

The sight of it, red, wet, and shiny, made TJ feel a familiar panic. Blood was meant to stay inside of you, a secret you didn't need to know and that should never be shared. He slowed to a stop and averted his eyes.

Two cop cars came racing up the road, turned onto the property, and skidded to a stop at an angle. The cops jumped out, guns drawn. From the shelter of their doors, they started shouting at Griffin to drop his weapon.

Instead of obeying, Griffin pointed a knife at them. He started yelling, his voice arcing high with panic. "Watch out! Dwayne's behind you!"

And then TJ saw what Griffin was trying to tell them. Dwayne, his hands cuffed in front of him, was sneaking up behind the cops.

When Griffin didn't drop the knife, one of the cops fired two bullets in quick succession. The first hit Griffin where his neck met his shoulder. TJ winced at the spray of blood it released. As Griffin fell to his knees, the knife dropped from his hand. The second shot just missed him as he tumbled face-first into the dirt.

Cheyenne was screaming Griffin's name. Her dark, sightless eyes were huge as she turned her head back and forth.

Dwayne was now just a few feet behind the nearest cop, who was still only focused on Griffin. Dwayne raised his cuffed hands high as he got ready to loop them over the cop's head and then yank back, strangling him.

It was becoming clear to TJ what would happen next. Dwayne would use the dying cop as a shield, he would take his gun, he would kill the other cop, and he would eventually get one of their handcuff keys and free himself. Along the way, he would kill everyone, most likely including TJ, all while wearing the same smile he had when he burned Cheyenne's hand.

TJ hurried to Griffin's body. He turned sideways and squatted until the fingers of his cuffed hand grazed one of the two guns the boy had stashed in the back of his pants. He stepped in front of Cheyenne, still turned at an angle, his body hiding the gun from the two cops. Behind him, he steadied his gun hand by curling his left hand around it and pointed it at Dwayne. If he hit one of the cops, so be it.

He just knew he had to stop Dwayne.

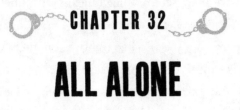

CHAPTER 32

ALL ALONE

CHEYENNE

Cheyenne lay with her body across Jaydra's, trying to shelter her from whatever awful things were happening around them. Bullets were flying in all directions. One of them seemed to have found Griffin.

"Griffin? Are you all right?" she yelled, but there was no answer.

She pressed one hand against the plastic bag that was supposed to be keeping the air out of Jaydra's lung. Cheyenne would not let herself think about how still Jaydra was. About how she hadn't even groaned when Cheyenne threw herself across her when the shooting started.

With her free hand, she groped desperately for Griffin. Was he dead or dying too?

All she found was fresh blood. The air was thick with oily smoke, and it seemed, if possible, to be even hotter than before. Was the Escalade on fire?

"Griffin!" she screamed. She sucked in a breath to call again, but the air scoured her lungs, leaving her coughing and gagging. She had to get Jaydra even farther away from the fire, but she also had to figure out what was happening. "Griffin? Talk to me!"

Feet ran through the gravel to her. Strong hands grabbed her arms and pulled her upright. "You're safe now, Cheyenne," a man said. She didn't recognize his voice.

She was just opening her mouth to answer when an explosion knocked them both sideways into the gravel.

Not knowing how much time had passed, Cheyenne pushed herself up to a sitting position. Her cheek stung. Her mouth was open, and she felt herself screaming, her vocal cords straining, her lips stretching, the air pushing out past them.

But what she heard was . . . nothing.

Nothing at all.

She was deaf.

Now she had neither eyes nor ears. It was like she was drifting soundlessly in space, all alone, with nothing to anchor her.

And Octavio was dead, and Duke. Griffin and Jaydra had to be dead, too.

And all because of her.

CHAPTER 33

MORE THAN SCARS

CHEYENNE

Eight hours later, Cheyenne sat by Griffin's hospital bed, waiting for him to wake up from surgery. The surgeon had told her and Griffin's aunt Debby that his wound wasn't life-threatening. The bullet had entered near his left shoulder, tunneled under the skin, and exited his right upper chest, near the base of the neck. It was a good thing, the surgeon said, that it had missed the subclavian vasculature.

Cheyenne didn't really know what that meant, but she did understand when he said Griffin should heal without anything more than a couple of dime-sized scars to show for it.

She was also just thankful she could hear what the surgeon said at all.

It turned out that the heat from the fire had caused one of the Escalade's tires to explode. When it did, it had been like she and the cop who was trying to help her were standing next to a bomb.

For the first five minutes, Cheyenne hadn't been able to hear anything. It had been her worst fear come to life. She completely lost it, sitting on the gravel screaming and crying and swearing, and hearing not a single sound. It felt like after the car accident, when she realized she was never going to see again. Like waking up in a locked coffin. Trapped in a smothering dark box while the world went on without her, even as she hammered on the lid and shouted to be let out—and no one heard her. When the second cop had grabbed her forearms, trying to help her up, she had freaked out even more at another pair of hands coming out of nowhere.

Then slowly she had begun to hear a faint trickle of sounds, overlaid with high-pitched squeals and hums. Now the ringing had mostly faded.

On the bed, she heard Griffin stir.

"Hello," he said softly, drawing out the word.

"Griffin!" She grabbed his good hand. "You're going to be okay. That's what the doctors say. How do you feel?"

"Fine. Basically. I mean, you're here and I'm not dead." His voice was slow and sleepy sounding. "And neither one of us is in handcuffs. What more could a guy ask for?" He squeezed her hand, then took a deep breath. "What about Jaydra?"

She squeezed back. "My dad and Danielle are with her. She's down the hall. She's in serious condition, but the doctors think she's going to make it."

"If Jaydra has anything to say about it, I'm sure she will."

Cheyenne had to smile at that. "Your aunt Debby just went to the cafeteria to grab some food. She should be back soon." At first, Debby had been wary around her, but the hours waiting for everyone to get out of surgery and recovery had broken down the wall between them.

"What about Dwayne?"

"He's dead," Cheyenne said. "TJ shot him with his own gun. Even though TJ was still wearing handcuffs."

"TJ always liked trick shots."

"The cops almost shot him, too, but I guess he threw the gun down after he shot Dwayne."

"He's probably more used to hearing 'drop your weapon' than I am." Griffin laughed, which turned into a cough, which turned into a coughing fit.

Cheyenne stood up. "Want me to get you some water?"

In a half-strangled voice, Griffin said, "I want something, but that's not it."

She loosened her fingers from his grasp and began to run them over the bed rail. Was he in pain? "Should I ring the nurse?"

"That's still not it." He cleared his throat, then pushed

a button. She felt the head of the bed move higher until he was mostly sitting up. He pressed another button, and the bed rail hummed down. Then he caught her hand and tugged. "Come here."

Cheyenne perched on the side of the bed, facing Griffin. Her heart was beating really fast, and she was suddenly glad that she had heard Debby close the door to the hall until it clicked shut.

Griffin put his good hand on the back of her neck and gently pulled her closer. Then his mouth was on hers, lightly at first, their noses bumping.

Cheyenne cupped his cheek and then ran her fingertips over the stubble on his jaw. She started to slide her hand to the back of his warm neck, but when she touched a bandage, she switched direction. Her fingers slipped into his soft, wavy hair. Under her lips, she felt him suck in his breath.

Suddenly they were kissing so hard it was like they were trying to merge into one person. Everything went into the kiss: the fear, the bravery, the longing, the joy.

Griffin turned his head for a second, breaking contact. "Wow!" he gasped.

And then he put his mouth back on Cheyenne's.

CHAPTER 34

NEVER WAVERING

GRIFFIN

"All rise!" said the bailiff.

Griffin got to his feet. A bubble expanded in his chest, crowding his lungs. This was it. His dad was finally facing his day of reckoning. At least for some things.

The trial had been postponed two weeks to allow Griffin time to recover, and for the prosecutor to determine what to do about the latest attempt to kidnap Cheyenne. Ultimately, Bennett had decided it would be too hard to present a winning case against Roy for what Dwayne and TJ had done. The authorities had found Roy's cell phone, and while they guessed that the half brothers had been in touch, there was no way to prove that Roy had played a role in what had happened. Dwayne was dead, and TJ was still considered incompetent to stand trial. That also meant no one would pay for the death of Octavio Ortiz.

TJ had told the cops that Octavio thought that they were planning to steal the Wilders' art collection. Dwayne had offered him a share of mythical millions. When Octavio realized the real plan was to steal Cheyenne, he had said no. And paid for it with his life.

With Octavio out of the picture, Dwayne had gone with his backup plan, persuading Cheyenne that he was Griffin. Although Griffin had asked what they had messaged each other, Cheyenne didn't want to share in any detail what she had said to Dwayne when she thought he was Griffin. He was super curious, but he didn't push.

TJ had been put back in Oregon State Hospital, and the fence around the yard had been reinforced with a second perimeter. Two of the workers who were supposed to have been watching the inmates the evening TJ escaped had been fired.

Now Judge Satterwhite, a tall black man with silvering hair, settled into his place at the front of the courtroom. "All right," he said. "Be seated, please."

Aunt Debby patted Griffin's knee as they settled back down. Cheyenne, who was on his other side, gave Griffin's hand a quick squeeze. He could pay attention to neither. His gaze was focused on his dad, who sat at the defense table with rigid shoulders. Between the suit and the haircut, it was almost possible to believe that this man was a stranger.

As Griffin waited for the verdict, his gut felt like someone had taken a weed whacker to it. Two days ago, he had testified against Roy. Against Bennett's advice, he looked his dad straight in the eye when he spoke, his voice never wavering.

In his dreams last night, Griffin had been sitting on this same hard bench, waiting for the jury to announce his father's fate. But something had kept happening to delay it: an earthquake, a fire drill, a microphone that didn't work.

The judge looked out at the crowded courtroom. This trial had everything the media loved: money, beauty, betrayal. Cheyenne represented both money and beauty. Griffin was betrayal.

"Let the record reflect that all parties in the trial are present and the jury is seated." Judge Satterwhite turned to the foreman. "Mr. Michaelson, has the jury reached a verdict?"

As all eyes swung to him, the foreman got to his feet. He swallowed before answering. "Yes, we have, Your Honor."

"Can you please state it?"

Michaelson kept his gaze on the judge. "We, the jury, find the defendant Roy Sawyer guilty of the offense of first-degree kidnapping as charged in the indictment."

"No!" Roy shouted. He banged his fist on the table and

then started to get up. Wheeler, his lawyer, yanked him back down, but not before the two sheriff's deputies started forward, their hands on their guns.

Cheyenne shrank back, her features bunching up. Now it was Griffin's turn to pat Cheyenne's knee and get no response. From the other side of Cheyenne, her dad, Nick, shot him a look. He pulled his hand back and adjusted his sling.

"Sir, will you be silent, please," the judge said in a steely tone. It wasn't a question.

It was Roy's lawyer who answered. "Sorry, Your Honor," Wheeler said. "It won't happen again."

His dad managed to keep quiet as the jury foreman repeated the word *guilty* over and over to the long list of charges related to Cheyenne's kidnapping: assault, abduction, unlawful restraint, and more.

Finally it was over. The judge thanked the jury. The deputies stepped forward to lead Roy away. Now that they were all on their feet, Griffin realized Bennett was right. At some point, he had gotten taller than his dad.

Their eyes met. Neither of their expressions changed, but somehow Griffin felt that his dad finally saw him for who he was. For the man he was becoming.

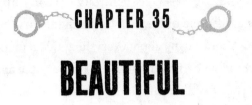

CHAPTER 35

BEAUTIFUL

CHEYENNE

It was the morning of Christmas Eve, and in some ways it had been like every Christmas season Cheyenne had ever known. In the foyer, a huge fir filled the air with its clean, spicy scent. Whenever the front door opened, the breeze rustled the silver tinsel and antique handblown glass stars that had decorated it every year that she could remember. When Danielle married Nick, she had made it clear to Cheyenne that she would never mess with important traditions.

But she had added some traditions of her own: homemade gingerbread cookies baked the first week of December, scented candles lined up on the mantelpiece, and Dutch babies served on Christmas Eve morning. These were cooked by Danielle herself and accompanied by melted butter, freshly squeezed lemon juice, and drifts of powdered sugar.

As Danielle carried the pancakes into the dining room, Griffin said, "That smells delicious." Having him at the table was just one of the things that made this Christmas unique. After hearing about everything that had happened and meeting Griffin themselves, Nick and Danielle had slowly changed their minds about him. And they had realized that, while the world was a risky place, they couldn't keep Cheyenne wrapped up and tucked away. They had to trust her to take care of herself and to make good decisions.

"You know what else smells delicious? Violet." Cheyenne sniffed the top of her sleeping sister's head and then kissed it. The baby didn't stir in her arms. She was only ten days old and was tightly wrapped in a cotton blanket, like an eight-pound burrito.

"It's the baby shampoo," her dad said.

"Maybe that's part of it," Cheyenne answered. "But some of it's just Violet. People want to act as if human beings don't have a smell, but we do. If you blindfolded me and put earplugs in my ears and lined up everyone I care about in front of me, I'll bet I could tell all of you apart just by sniffing."

"I believe you." Danielle set a plate in front of her. "We're all still animals at heart."

Maybe she was thinking of Violet's birth. Cheyenne had gotten to be in the delivery room. Even without being able to see it, the birth was an incredibly intimate and moving experience. Sometimes primal and scary. Right before the baby was born, Danielle screamed as she crushed Cheyenne's hand. At the end of the hospital bed, Nick shouted encouragement. And a few minutes later, the baby slid into the doctor's hands and let out a cry.

"Here, let me hold her." Her dad got up and took Violet from Cheyenne's arms. "I have more practice than you do at eating while holding a sleeping infant. It reminds me of the early days with your mom, when the baby was you." His voice thickened with emotion. Something about Violet's birth seemed to have freed him and Cheyenne to talk about her mom more than they had since she died. He cleared his throat and then changed the subject. "I heard from Jaydra yesterday. It sounds like she's got herself a new gig."

Jaydra had spent the summer on Nick's payroll, not as a bodyguard, but just to recover from her wound and regain her strength. The doctors credited her full recovery to her peak physical condition. Cheyenne was sure Jaydra's stubbornness must also have been a big factor. No one ever really said no to Jaydra, and that included her body.

"What's she going to be doing?" Cheyenne asked. There were rumors that an unauthorized TV movie of their ordeal was in the works, with the reigning female MMA fighter starring as Jaydra.

"She wouldn't exactly spell it out. But I wouldn't be

surprised if someday we see her standing right behind the president with a mic in her ear."

"Secret Service?" Cheyenne asked. It was fun to imagine Jaydra bossing the president around.

"If I told you, then it wouldn't be so secret, would it?" Her dad laughed at his own joke.

"She would kill at that," Griffin said. "Maybe literally."

For a moment, there was only the sound of people eating. Cheyenne's mouth filled with the zing of lemon, the silkiness of melted butter, and the sweetness of powdered sugar layered on the puffy pancake.

Then Danielle asked, "So, Griffin, are you done with school this term?"

"Yeah. I actually think I did pretty well." Surprise colored his voice.

Griffin had taken two art classes at Portland Community College, which didn't require that he have a high school diploma to attend. Danielle had looked into it, though, and it turned out there were ways to get a GED even when you had trouble reading, the way Griffin did. Cheyenne's dad had arranged a job for him at the Nike outlet store, and he now shared an apartment with two other employees.

"In fact, Nick and Danielle," Griffin said, "my final project was actually meant as a gift for you guys. To thank you for everything you've done for me."

"You didn't have to do that," Danielle said.

"I did it because I wanted to. It's in my backpack in the entryway—is it okay if I go get it?"

"Of course," Nick said. Cheyenne heard the curiosity in his voice. She was intrigued, too, but of course, without sight, most art was sealed away from her. She had been to a museum just once since she had gone blind, one she had been to before. She had listened to the audio guide, relying on a combination of imagination and memory to know what the paintings looked like. And even then it was just a guess.

Griffin scooted his chair back. When he returned, staccato footfalls accompanied him.

"Duke wanted in," Griffin called out. "I hope that's okay."

"Anything Duke wants, Duke gets. You know that," her dad said. He had found Duke gravely injured near the self-driving car. Duke's front left leg had had to be amputated, leaving him with a hopping gait. In an odd way, the injury seemed to have mellowed him. He could no longer rely on his fierce physicality to navigate the world.

Cheyenne heard the backpack's zipper unzip, and then Griffin pulled something free. There was a crackle of paper as he unwrapped it.

Danielle sucked in a breath. "Oh, that's beautiful!"

Her dad said, "Wow!"

Griffin put it into Cheyenne's hands. It was a flat rectangle about the size of a tabloid sheet of paper.

"Go ahead," Griffin urged. "You can touch it."

The back was smooth and felt like pressboard. "What is it?" she asked, running her fingers around the edges of a narrow wooden frame. She gingerly moved her fingertips to the front. It was hard and bumpy with texture.

"It's an oil painting," he said. "I've been playing around with putting the paint on really thick, so maybe you could see it that way."

"What's the subject?" At the top were thick swirls, but the rest of the painting was smoother.

"Can you guess?"

Near the center of the painting, her fingers found a round dot about as big as a thumbprint. There was another dot parallel with the first, about two inches away. She checked out the swirls again, and then the dots. Above each dot was an arch as wide as a pencil. Eyebrows, she suddenly thought. Eyebrows and eyes and curly hair.

"Is it a portrait?" she asked.

"It's you," Danielle said softly in what Cheyenne had come to think of as her mom voice. "It's a portrait of you. And it's beautiful."

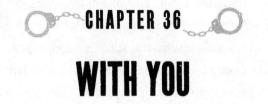

CHAPTER 36

WITH YOU

CHEYENNE

The dogs raced ahead of Cheyenne and Griffin as they ventured out into the backyard. It had started to snow while they were eating breakfast, and judging by the sound it made under their shoes, an inch or so had accumulated. If the snow stuck around until tomorrow, it would be Portland's first white Christmas in their lifetimes. Snow was rare in the city. If it came at all, it was usually after the first of the year.

Cheyenne had one arm looped through Griffin's. She smiled as she heard Duke and Phantom scuttle and chase, stop and start, snuffle and snort, and sometimes even bite the snow. Phantom worked so hard that it was good to hear him play. Aside from the dogs and the sound of their footsteps, the world was hushed. The frosty air tasted clean.

"Can you use your cane in the snow?" Griffin asked.

"Only a couple of times, before I got Phantom. I don't like it. Normally, I can tell what things are just by the sound they make when my cane touches them, but in the snow, everything sounds the same. If you don't pay attention, it's super easy to get lost. And you have to be careful not to get the tip of the cane stuck." She squeezed his arm. "Good thing I've got you to guide me."

Griffin squeezed back. "You're welcome." Then he sighed. "Too bad I'm going to have to go pretty soon if I want to make my bus." He was scheduled to work the afternoon shift at the Nike outlet, catering to last-minute Christmas shoppers.

"I can't wait until April," Cheyenne said. That was the month when the self-driving cars were scheduled to go into production. She was seventh in line. "Then I'll be able to drive you home. Or let the car drive both of us."

She heard the smile in Griffin's voice. "And the nice thing about the car is that you won't have to worry about keeping your eyes on the road and your hands on the wheel."

"Hmm," she teased, "why do you say that like it's a good thing?"

He stopped walking and pulled her close. She let herself be gathered into his arms, but didn't kiss him. "Can my dad and Danielle see us?" she asked.

Griffin shifted. "I can see the living room windows from here, but I can't see them." Still, he released her.

The air changed, becoming closer. Then, with the lightest of touches, flakes began to land on Cheyenne's cheeks and forehead. She tilted her head and stuck out her tongue until she felt one land, a faint, soft cold that disappeared even as she felt it.

"I wish it snowed more often," Griffin said. "I like how it makes everything clean and new and soft."

"When I was a kid, it felt magical to step on fresh snow," Cheyenne said. "Like you were an explorer stepping into another country."

"I feel like that with you all the time," Griffin said softly. "Like I'm someplace completely familiar and yet totally new. All at the same time."

Without a word, Cheyenne slipped into his arms. She no longer cared if anyone was watching. Griffin's mouth was warm, and under his lips, she felt herself melting.

ACKNOWLEDGMENTS

When I wrote Girl, Stolen in 2008, I never intended to write a sequel. Never say never, because a great idea might just come along.

The research for this book was fascinating. In the intervening years, a lot of technology has been developed (especially for the smartphone) that can help people who are blind.

Richard Turner, MSW, training center director for the Oregon Commission for the Blind, showed me several cool apps and gadgets and patiently answered my many questions. He put me in touch with his co-worker Angel Hale, director of vocational rehabilitation services, who shared with me all kinds of tricks she uses to keep herself and her house looking good. She even recommended the brand of eye shadow I now use! And Kody Keplinger, author of *The Duff* and *Run*, helped me understand more about what it's like to have a guide dog.

When it comes to self-defense for the blind, I'd like to thank Sensei Stan Miller for letting me observe the Sightless Self-Defense class, which he developed. Stephen Nicholls, the director of 1Touch, a London-based self-defense program for the blind, and Miranda Brown, its executive administrative assistant, actually managed to meet with me in Portland. They even fine-tuned and then acted out a climactic scene for me in the lobby of a DoubleTree Hotel (to the amusement of passersby).

I would also like to thank the many martial arts instructors I have had over the years: Sifu Kevin Warren, a black belt in kajukenbo; Sifu Wally Jones, a black belt in kung fu and a blue belt in Brazilian jujitsu; Coach Chris Bauer, a brown belt in Brazilian jujitsu; and Professor Bill Bradley, a black belt in Brazilian jujitsu.

Jaydra Perfetti, a brown belt in kung fu, let me borrow her first name and her badass spirit. And Kevin Reeve from onPoint Tactical taught me how to get out of handcuffs, duct tape, zip ties, and rope, as well as how to pick locks, steal cars, and other tricks every mystery writer should know.

Gabe Nelson, a reporter for *Automotive News*, helped me speculate about the future of self-driving cars. Prosecutor Paul Parisi answered questions about how a prosecutor would prepare witnesses for an upcoming trial. Former cop and author Robin Burcell advised me in many ways large and small. Joe Collins, a paramedic and firefighter, assisted me in setting my own fictional fire. Pathologist Judy Melinek, MD, who is also the author of *Working Stiff*, answered my questions about gunshot wounds.

I'm the luckiest girl in the world, because this is my twenty-first book with my agent, Wendy Schmalz, and my seventh with editor Christy Ottaviano, whose voice I now sometimes hear in my head when I'm writing. Jessica Anderson helps keep the wheels on the bus. April Ward designs my amazing covers. Molly Brouillette can coordinate events across a half dozen states and then offer a shoulder to cry on when a crucial flight is canceled. Other wonderful folks at Henry Holt include Lucy Del Priore, Katie Halata, Melissa Croce, Jennifer Healey, Allison Verost, and Mark Von Bargen.